The Penguin Poets
The Penguin Book of Modern

Mahmood Jamal was born in Lucknow, India, in 1948 and came to Britain from Pakistan in 1967. For several years he was a regular participant in Black Voices, a forum for Third World writers, and his poems have been published in the **London Magazine**, **Black Phoenix** and **Poetry Round**, and in several anthologies of Third World poetry. In 1976 his work was published along with that of three other poets in a volume entitled **Coins for Charon**. His poems have been broadcast on Radio London, Radio 3 and BBC TV and have been translated into several languages including Turkish and Urdu.

In 1984 Mahmood Jamal was the recipient of the Minority Rights Group award for his poetry, translations and critical writing. He has written and researched several documentary films, including the controversial **Living in Danger** which was shown on Channel 4. He has also directed two documentary films. He currently works for Retake Film and Video Collective, of which he was a founder member. In 1984 his first volume of poetry, **Silence Inside a Gun's Mouth**, was published. Mr Jamal has a degree in South Asian Studies from the School of Oriental and African Studies, University of London.

THE PENGUIN BOOK OF MODERN URDU POETRY

Selected and translated by Mahmood Jamal

Penguin Books

Penguin Books Ltd, Harmondsworth, Middlesex, England
Viking Penguin Inc., 40 West 23rd Street, New York, New York 10010, U.S.A.
Penguin Books Australia Ltd, Ringwood, Victoria, Australia
Penguin Books Canada Limited, 2801 John Street, Markham, Ontario, Canada
L3R 1B4
Penguin Books (N.Z.) Ltd, 182–190 Wairau Road, Auckland 10, New Zealand

First published 1986

Designed by Paul McAlinden

Made and printed in Great Britain by
Cox & Wyman Ltd, Reading
Typeset in Linotron Bodoni by
Rowland Phototypesetting Ltd, Bury St Edmunds, Suffolk

CONTENTS

Contents

ACKNOWLEDGEMENTS

I would like to thank all the poets, friends and well-wishers whose cooperation and advice made this work possible. In particular, I wish to thank Dr Akhtar Husain Raipuri, whose enthusiasm, support and criticism were a great influence on me; Mr Ralph Russell, Mr Naiyer Masud Rizvi of Lucknow University; Mr Abdul Rab of Uttar Pradesh Urdu Academy; Mr Iftiqar Arif of the Urdu Markaz; Miss Shabana Mahmud of the India Office Library, London; Dr Humayun Ansari; Mr Ahmad Faraz; Mr Saqi Farooqi; Mr Allister Goulding, who gave me invaluable support through his comments, editorial suggestions and organizational help; and finally Mr Abdullah-al-Udhari, poet and translator, who gave me useful advice on translation and encouraged me to undertake this work.

The poems by Faiz Ahmad Faiz are published by courtesy of the Faiz Foundation. I am grateful to all the writers whose poems are included in this volume, and to their publishers, for permission to use their work here.

INTRODUCTION

Urdu, like English, is a hybrid language, and came into existence at about the same time.

As the word Urdu suggests (it is a Turkish word meaning 'army camp' or 'horde'), the language developed out of the interaction between the local population of northern India and the conquering Muslims from central Asia who began to settle there in the twelfth and thirteenth centuries.

As a written language, Urdu took its distinct form in the seventeenth century though its literature can be traced back to the fourteenth. Since its roots lay in the Arabized Persian of the conquering Muslims, it inherited the highly developed diction of Persian literature. At the same time, it was able to incorporate in itself the rustic simplicity of Hindi or Khari Boli and other regional dialects of India, thus acquiring a range and contrast well suited to poetic expression.

Since Muslims settled mainly in towns, Urdu developed as a predominantly urban language, though its links with regional spoken languages make it accessible in its spoken form to the rural population. After the decline of the Moghuls and the consolidation of British power over northern India as a whole, Urdu replaced Persian as the official language. This fact, coupled with the dominance of Muslim nobility, made it possible for Urdu literature to acquire a central position in Indian cultural life. It was only in the twentieth century that its predominance was challenged by emerging Hindu nationalism, and the political gulf that divided the Muslims from the Hindu majority also separated Urdu from Hindi. After the partition of India, Urdu was adopted as the national language of Pakistan while in India it was replaced by Hindi. (In speech the two languages are still almost identical, but Hindi uses a script derived from Sanskrit.)

One of the peculiarities of Urdu is that, in spite of its being one of the most widely spoken languages of the sub-continent, it has no home in any province. In Uttar Pradesh, where it mainly developed, it is considered the language of the

Muslim minority. In Pakistan, where it is the national language, only a small proportion of the population consider it their mother tongue. None the less, in both India (in the form of Hindustani) and in Pakistan, Urdu remains the lingua franca.

Part of the credit for the popularity and accessibility of Urdu must go to the Indian cinema. Though the language was much diluted and often vulgarized in cheap dialogue and film songs, it was the cinema which made even village India come to terms with Urdu. The participation of many Urdu writers and poets in the Bombay film industry helped to make Urdu a language both of literature and of popular speech – which in turn facilitated its usage in politics; many of the slogans and poems sung by political activists are evidence of its universality.

Urdu literature emerged from a sophisticated Persian tradition. Used neither for commerce nor for law, it was not a utilitarian language. Before the middle of the nineteenth century Urdu literature consisted almost entirely of poetry, the models coming from Persian. The bulk of Urdu poetry was made up of *gazals* (love lyrics), though other forms such as *masnavis* (narrative poems), *qasidas* (panegyrics) and *rubaiyat* (quatrains) also flourished.

There was not much in Urdu *gazal* writing which could be described as political or social. Nevertheless, varied subjects of philosophical and psychological importance were dealt with in great depth and with astounding beauty of expression. After the demise of the last Moghul emperor, Bahadur Shah (himself a poet, in whose court the last great flowering of traditional Urdu verse took place through the work of Ghalib, Zauq and Momin), Urdu poetry entered a stagnant period and slid into decadence, ornamentation and decline as Muslim kingdoms tottered and collapsed under the British onslaught.

The expansion of British rule and its rapid westward advance from Bengal did not, however, go unchallenged. In 1857 northern India was caught in a desperate uprising which shook the foundations of the British Raj. The rebellion – a last-ditch effort to re-establish the last Moghul emperor as ruler of India – failed, but it forced Muslim thinkers to examine the causes of Muslim decline.

The most important and influential person to emerge in this field after the events of 1857 was a Muslim scholar, Syed Ahmad Khan (1817–98), who, through his close contact with the British, took a critical view of the Muslim community. Having witnessed the power of the British and become convinced of their invincibility, he exhorted the Muslims to come to terms with the Raj. Almost single-handed he started a movement for reform (later known as the Aligarh Movement) in the Muslim community, which gave birth to a didactic and reformist trend in Urdu literature. His articles and essays, coupled with the letters of the great poet Ghalib (1797–1869), form the basis of modern Urdu prose.

Syed Ahmad Khan was more concerned with social reform than with literature. It was in his disciple and successor, Altaf Husain Hali (1837–1914), that modern Urdu literature found its theoretician. Hali, who was both poet and critic, took Urdu poetry out of its introversion and obsession with ornamentation and form, and used it to tackle political and social themes.

Around the turn of the century Muhammad Iqbal (1873–1938) further changed the form and content of Urdu poetry, though retaining a traditional idiom and framework. Josh Malihabadi (1896–1982), who bridges the age of Iqbal and the modern era of Urdu poetry, dragged Urdu verse out of the garden of *gazal* into the concrete plazas of twentieth-century India. Yet his style and diction remained fairly traditional and his language highly literary, although, to the ordinary listener, almost incomprehensible.

It was in the 1930s that Urdu poetry reached another turning-point. Poets facing the trauma of colonial oppression began to reflect this in their work. Mass politics were emerging through the Indian freedom movement. Writers organized themselves in the Progressive Writers Association. The most important literary body in India, the PWA profoundly influenced the evolution of modern Urdu poetry; almost every major writer of Urdu was either a member of the movement or closely associated with it. Since Urdu poetry so easily lent itself to spoken expression, it was readily adaptable to political gatherings and rallies; in this period of Indian history Urdu became the main language of cultural resistance. Poetry left the courts of nobles and kings, the small literary circles and sprawling mansions where it had adored the maiden of some distant dream, and emerged violently and defiantly in public gatherings, in coffee-houses and in the pages of the newspapers and periodicals which were proliferating all over the sub-continent. Poets began to forge new poems to meet the changed and changing reality that faced them. Naturally, poetic form had to be adapted to the new task. Aesthetic and philosophical preoccupations that had been sustained by feudal wealth and easy living were seriously undermined. The inspiration for the new poets such as Faiz Ahmad Faiz and Ali Sardar J'afri no longer came from cruel lips and dark eyes, or from ancient kings and queens; it came instead from the concrete possibilities opened for mankind by the 1917 revolution. Of course the trauma of war, exploitation, and the influence of Russian and French literature also played their part. A much-needed dynamism had at last been injected and a new era had begun, different in form and content (though the traditional and popular form of *gazal* continued to flourish, as it does to this day).

What is both interesting and exciting is the way in which Urdu, locked in tradition and stasis, could so easily adapt itself to become a language of revolution, social comment and political action. One of the reasons for this is the symbolic nature of the language itself. Another is a tradition of rebellion and rejection of the status quo that runs through most mystical Urdu poetry. Because of its symbolic nature, Urdu poetry is open to a multiplicity of interpretations; ambiguity is almost an essential quality.

The traditional symbols of Urdu poetry – *majnoon* (mad lover), *saqi* (wine-giver), *dar* (gallows), martyrdom and blood, the oppressor's sword, the indifferent loved one – all occur in this transitional phase of modern Urdu literature and maintain their freshness and potency. This is because it is not the words themselves that are powerful, but their context and association which give them strength. In an age of nationalist struggle and social change, the mad lover became the rebel or revolutionary, the gallows became a symbol of the cruelty of the rulers and the martyrdom of the political activist. As in mystical Urdu poetry symbols could be both secular and religious, the beloved being both God and a human being, so in revolutionary Urdu poetry the beloved could be one's country or a person; and the wine-giver could become a cruel dictator.

Although this enabled Urdu poetry to meet the new challenge without much difficulty, it had a drawback. While the form remained traditional, the content raced ahead and exhausted itself. Because of the tremendous weight of tradition in both literature and society, innovations in Urdu poetry have tended to be partial. The work of Faiz Ahmad Faiz and others of his generation – and of even later poets such as Faraz – is often laden with traditional imagery. But in N.M.Rashed (a contemporary of Faiz) and recently in Saqi Farooqi, Amiq Hanafi and Munir Niazi, one can see a more definitive break with traditional form and subject-matter.

It was, however, in its more traditional and only partly modern form that Urdu poetry became popular. The most important and popularly acclaimed poet of modern Urdu literature, from his first impact in the 1930s and 1940s until his death in 1984, was Faiz Ahmad Faiz. His strength lay in the subtle blending of romance and idealism, simple diction and accessible images, and, above all, in his desire to reach the masses and his concern for humanity. He hardly ever wrote free verse and maintained a certain rhythm and metre, often using the *gazal* to convey a political message as no poet had done before him. The cultural scene in which he operated was not ready to accommodate a total break with the past. Yet his contemporary, N.M.Rashed, tried precisely that and became the first real modernist of Urdu literature. Rashed wrote in free verse and introduced new subjects. His poetry was essentially for reading from the page; in a society where literacy is abysmally low and publishing tremendously difficult, it was doomed to reach only a fairly small circle of admirers.

Rashed, because of his rather apolitical stance and his own artistic uniqueness, not only shocked many readers but managed to alienate himself from the progressive writers of his generation. He must, however, stand as an innovator and there are critics who place him on the same level as Faiz, and even higher. His contribution was to break down the very relationships between words that had typified earlier forms and to evolve and experiment with new forms and structures. In this he was the first of his kind in Urdu poetry, giving birth to a parallel trend to that started by Faiz – Rashed, too, has his followers in poets such as Saqi Farooqi and Amiq Hanafi. Akhtar-ul-Iman, a contemporary of Faiz and Rashed, used a modernist style and everyday language to deal with subjects hitherto untouched by Urdu verse. These three, together with Miraji and Ali Sardar J'afri, were to influence subsequent generations of poets in varying degrees and are considered the fathers of modern Urdu poetry – though Faiz's popularity and domination of the poetic landscape after partition was undisputed on both sides of the border. Two of the most popular and acclaimed poems of modern Urdu, 'Freedom's Dawn' and

'Do Not Ask of Me, My Love', were written by Faiz and have influenced most younger writers.

If Faiz, Rashed, Miraji and Akhtar-ul-Iman are held to be the most important poets, Ali Sardar J'afri is considered the leading intellectual of the literary world. His importance as a poet lies both in his critical and theoretical writing, and in the way in which he brought revolutionary ideas and fervour into his work. Though his poems often lack the subtlety of Faiz, they are in no way lacking in revolutionary sentiment and modern vocabulary. As the leading light of the Progressive Writers Association, Ali Sardar J'afri was certainly one of the people responsible for reclaiming Urdu poetry and giving it a socialist aesthetic; the credit for the emergence of revolutionary Urdu poetry must to a large extent go to him.

To put into its proper perspective the kind of poetry that Sardar J'afri and, later, Habib Jalib have produced, an important point must be made about the role of progressive Urdu poets and their work in the cultural and political life of post-partition India. In Pakistan, which has suffered several military dictatorships, their courage and creativity has been exemplary. Unlike their Western counterparts, Urdu poets have enjoyed a prominence and popularity only accorded in the West to filmstars and pop musicians. A public *mushaira* or poetry reading can easily attract tens of thousands of people, many of whom are often illiterate, yet sophisticated enough to applaud the subtle turn of phrase or political allusion in a poem. When you can attract the attention of so many through verse you cannot remain aloof from politics, particularly when dictators, propped up by foreign aid programmes, feel nervous and shaky at any assembly where people can speak freely. Imprisonment may seem an incongruous subject to those who are used to a poetry which addresses only intellectuals and academics; but if we glance at the important names of post-war Urdu poetry, we can find hardly any major poet who has escaped jail. Faiz suffered imprisonment

17

and later, under another military dictatorship, a long period of exile. Ahmad Faraz and Habib Jalib, two of the most popular Urdu poets of today, have both been in prison and Faraz is now living in exile in Britain. Even in India, the eyes and wrath of 'democratic' institutions have fallen on certain poets. Ali Sardar J'afri was incarcerated in the early fifties. Going further back, two major Urdu poets were targets for the British. Hasrat Mohani was sentenced to rigorous imprisonment; and Josh Malihabadi's famous poem, 'To the Heirs of the East India Company', was banned for fear of what it might do to the British war effort.

Most of the poets who went to prison did not stop writing; indeed, some produced their best works there. Like Kim Chi Ha in Korea, Nazim Hikmet in Turkey, Said Zahiri in Singapore and Yanis Ritsos in Greece, they refused to be silenced and sounded a warning to all dictators:

Those who brew the poison of cruelty
will not win, tomorrow or today.
They can put out the lamps
where lovers meet;
they cannot blind the moon!

(Faiz, 'A Prison Nightfall')

All this attention from rulers is an indication of the importance Urdu poets have enjoyed in the hearts and minds of the public. Though open and free *mushairas* are now banned in Pakistan, poetry enjoys an undiminished popularity. When the time comes, once again thousands will assemble to hear a Faraz, or a Jalib, give voice to the throbbing in their hearts.

In my hand I hold a pen,
in my heart the light of consciousness.
How can your forces of oppression
ever win?

(Jalib, 'On the Banning of a Book of Poems')

The poems I have chosen for this volume are a reflection
of the various trends, both dominant and secondary, that have
been present in Urdu poetry since the thirties. The euphoric era
of the forties (when India was partitioned into two separate
states) was to lead into a period of disappointment and despair
when the new rulers of the sub-continent were unable to deliver
the people from misery. Poets turned to sloganizing to arouse the
people to revolt, and some, disillusioned by the failure of their
own ideology, began to explore more personal areas of life; a kind
of healthy scepticism emerged in Urdu poetry in the sixties. With
this trend poets became more speculative, introverted and
psychological in their themes. This brought a new and welcome
dimension to Urdu poetry, and slowly the powerful and often
dogmatic world of the Progressive Writers was weakened; the
sloganizing in which many of the best poets indulged was exposed
for what it was – propaganda rather than art.

Another important development in Urdu poetry since
the war has been the emergence of women poets. Urdu poetry as
a whole has been expanded and enriched by the subject-matter
and style of such poets as Fahmida Riaz and Kishwar Naheed.
Women writers are now firmly on the scene and – in spite of
chauvinistic obstacles to their full expression – will continue to be
an important force, as the poems included here, by the two
leading women poets of today, will testify.

Finally, I would like to add that the poems and poets
chosen for this volume do not at all constitute a total
representation of twentieth-century Urdu poetry; for this a much
larger volume is required. The most important figure deliberately
omitted here is Josh Malihabadi, whose poetry, though very
modern in outlook, somehow falls outside modernism as I have
defined it. Josh Malihabadi occupies a no-man's-land between
Iqbal and Faiz and poses very difficult problems of translation.
He was a prolific writer who deserves separate attention, and he
certainly ranks with Iqbal and Faiz as a leading twentieth-

century poet. The works I have chosen are all by poets who have made some contribution to the development of modern Urdu poetry. Considerations of translatability, modernity and subject-matter have played a part in the selection. I have completely omitted the *gazal*, which almost every Urdu writer, both modern and traditional, has written with great effect and beauty. The twentieth-century *gazal* deserves a separate volume, and perhaps someone is already making efforts in this direction; *gazal* still has a powerful hold on the sub-continent because it can be sung with musical accompaniment.

As any anthology is subjective, so is this selection. Something of the original is always lost in translation (in the opinion of some, the most important part). In translation from a culture and tradition so distinct, the loss of context itself diminishes the beauty and depth of a poem. Yet I hope I have managed, through this slim volume, to give the reader a glimpse of modern Urdu poetry.

M.J.

FAIZ AHMAD FAIZ

1911–84:

Widely acclaimed as the leading twentieth-century Urdu poet, Faiz was born in Sialkot, Punjab, and had a varied career as teacher, army officer, journalist, political leader, trade unionist and broadcaster. His poems reached a wide audience through radio, and almost every popular singer has sung his *gazals*. The poems have been translated into several languages, including English; collections of his works have recently been published in Karachi and London. Imprisoned more than once by the Pakistani government for his political stance, he spent a period of exile with the Palestinians in Beirut. He returned to Pakistan in 1984, where he died in Lahore. Faiz received many literary awards, notably the Lenin Prize.

Nowhere, No Trace Can I Discover

Nowhere, no trace can I discover
of spilt blood,
not on the murderer's hand nor on his sleeve;
no daggers with red lips nor scarlet-pointed swords.
I see no blots on the dust,
no stains on the walls.

Nowhere, nowhere
does the blood reveal its darkness.

Not spilt in grandeur
nor as ritual sacrifice,
it was not shed on the field of battle,
it did not raise a martyr's banner.

Screaming loudly the orphan blood flowed on.
No-one had the time or sense,
none bothered to listen.

No witness, no defence;
the case is closed.
The blood of the downtrodden
seeped mutely into the dust.

My Guests

The door opens
on my sadness;
there they come, my guests.
There she is, the evening
to lay a carpet of despair.
There goes the night
to speak of pain to the stars.
Here comes the morning
with its shining scalpel
to open the wound of memory.
Then there is afternoon
hiding whips of flame in its sleeve.
All these are my guests
who come to see me day and night.
But when they come
and when they go,
I do not know.
My thoughts are always
drifting homeward,
holding doubts and suspicions,
asking many questions.

Poetry's Theme

The evening flickers, glows and falters to a halt.
The night will come, washed clean with moonlight.
And we shall speak again with gestures of our eyes,
and those hands will clasp these yearning hands of mine.

Is it her scarf, her face, her dress
that makes the veil so bright, so clear?
Does that earring glitter still
in the ambiguous dark shade of her hair?

Once again, her beauty will adorn the night:
those dreamy eyes, those lines of black,
that subtle hint of powder on her cheek,
that delicate line of henna on her palm –

This, if any, is my world of thought, my poetry;
this the soul of context, the heart of meaning.

What have Adam's luckless children suffered
in our cruel and bloody centuries?
What have our forefathers suffered?
What shall we suffer,
in the daily battle of life and death?
Why do these youthful and glamorous cities
live in the hope of merely dying?
Why does only hunger grow
in fields where harvests are blooming?

These mysterious frightening walls
within which so many lives have been snuffed out
each instant; these tortured dreams
whose glow still haunts the minds of millions –
These too are subjects of poetry
and there are many, many more.
But still –
those gently parting lips,

those wicked curves!
Tell me, friend:
is there a more alluring subject anywhere?

The subject of my verses is none else;
the home for a poet's heart is nowhere else!

The Smell of Blood

The smell of blood
or the fragrance of a lover's lips?
I wonder what the breeze
will bring for me
today.

Has spring arrived in the garden? Or
have the prisons found new inhabitants?
Where will the music come from today,
the sound of singing?

A Prison Nightfall

The night descends
step by silent step
down the stairway of stars.
The breeze goes by me
like a kindly whispered phrase.

The homeless trees of the prison yard
are absorbed, making patterns
against the sky.

On the roof's high crest
the loving hand of moonlight rests.
The starry river is drowned in dust
and the sky glows silver with moonlight.
In the dark foliage
shadows play with the wind
as a wave of painful loss
invades the heart.

Defiantly, a thought tells me
how sweet life is at this instant:
Those who brew the poison of cruelty
will not win, tomorrow or today.
They can put out the lamps
where lovers meet;
they cannot blind the moon!

Crosses

There are so many crosses
planted by my window
each carrying its own Christ
each yearning to meet his God.
On some the spring is sacrificed
on some the moon lies crucified
on some the fruitful branch is blinded
on some the morning breeze is slaughtered.
Each passing day
these blood-laced visions
come into my mind.
Each passing day, in front of me
their martyred bodies are
resurrected.

Scene

The street, shade, a tree, a house, a door,
a balcony.
On the balcony the moon reveals her breast
quietly
as someone gently taking off her dress.

Around the balcony, shadows gather,
a shadow stream.
On the stream a bubble floats from a leaf,
stops, moans, bursts gently, silently;
very gently the sweet colour of wine
dissolves in my glass, softly.

The glass of wine, the bottle,
the roses of your hands –
as in the background of thought
a dream casts a shadow,
forms itself into a pattern,
then quietly disintegrates.

The heart repeats a word of love, so softly.
You said 'Gently.'
The moon looked down
and said 'And still more gently.'

Encounters

1

The wall is blackened
by the night,
the streets snuffed out and dark,
the crowd has gone.
I will spend the night again
with my sole companion, solitude.
It seems that I must meet her once again –
she who carries on one palm henna,
on the other blood,
in one eye poison, in the other wine.

2

It's been so long since anyone
came into my heart.
In painful solitude
the garden of my heart has withered.
Who will fill with crimson
the chalice of my wounds?
And then,
without warning,
my waiting's over, she is there to greet me:
my friend death
who is an enemy and a consoler,
death who is our murderer and our lover.

Freedom's Dawn

This dawn that's marked and wounded,
this dawn that night has nibbled on –
It's not the dawn we expected;
it's not the dawn we were looking for.
Hoping we would find it somewhere
friends, comrades set out thinking
Somewhere in the desert of the sky
the stars would halt
Somewhere the night's slow waves
would find a shore
Somewhere the ship of our heartaches
come to rest.

When we set out on youth's mysterious journey
so many hands reached out to lure us back.
From the restless bedrooms in love's palace
so many embraces beckoned, bodies called.
But so much dearer was the face of dawn,
the dress of morning's maiden;
our dreams were stronger than our weariness.

But what is this we hear?
That all the battles have been fought,
that the destination has been reached!
It's all changed, our leaders' struggling zeal;
celebration is the order of the day, mourning forbidden.
Yet anguish of the heart, unfulfilled desire,
nothing is cured by this false dawn.
When did it come and where has it gone?
The lamp still waits for the morning breeze,
the night weighs on us still.
This is not the moment of our freedom.
Keep moving, keep moving!
We have not arrived!

To Those Palestinians Martyred in Foreign Lands

Sweet earth of Palestine,
wherever I went
carrying the burning scars of your humiliation,
nursing in my heart the longing
to make you proud,
your love, your memories went with me,
the fragrance of your orange groves went with me.

A crowd of unseen friends stood by me
and so many hands clasped mine.
In distant lands, on dark lanes,
in alien cities, on nameless streets,
wherever the banner of my blood unfurled,
I've left a Palestinian flag.
Your enemies destroyed one Palestine;
my wounds created many more.

Do Not Ask of Me, My Love

Do not ask of me, my love,
that love I once had for you.
There was a time when
life was bright and young and blooming,
and your sorrow was much more than
any other pain.
Your beauty gave the spring everlasting youth;
your eyes, yes your eyes were everything,
all else was vain.
While you were mine, I thought, the world was mine.
Though now I know that it was not reality,
That's the way I imagined it to be;
for there are other sorrows in the world than love,
and other pleasures, too.
Woven in silk and satin and brocade,
those dark and brutal curses of countless centuries:
bodies bathed in blood, smeared with dust,
sold from market-place to market-place,
bodies risen from the cauldron of disease
pus dripping from their festering sores –
my eyes must also turn to these.
You're beautiful still, my love
but I am helpless too;
for there are other sorrows in the world than love,
and other pleasures too.
Do not ask of me, my love,
that love I once had for you!

My City

What is the latest fashion in my city now?
What price does the spring extort these days?
Are they tearing out their hearts
in lonely streets
or does their empty morning start
inside the dungeon?
Are they in dreary drinking-houses
deep in wine?
Tell me! Tell me what my friends are suffering
in these troubled times!

When the Sorrow of My Heart

When the sorrow of my heart
came up and filled my eyes
I had no choice
but to listen to my friends' advice:
I washed my eyes
with blood.
Now every face and form
has turned to blood.
Blood red the golden sun
blood red the silver moon
blood red the morning's laughter
blood red the night's weeping;
every tree a column of blood
every flower a bloodied eye
every glance a sting of blood
every image flowing blood.
So long as this river of blood
keeps flowing
its colour is the red desire
of martyrdom, pain, anger and passion;
but if it is stopped
it twists and turns
with hatred, night and death,
the colour of mourning
for every colour.
Do not let this happen, friends:
bring me a flood of tears instead,
the pool
in which to wash this blood
this blood in my eyes
my blood-soaked eyes.

They Were the Lucky Ones

They were the lucky ones,
who worked a bit and loved a bit
who took loving as a task
or just loved their work.
I was rather busy too in my own way
I loved a little, worked a little.
The work disrupted my loving
and love often came in the way of work.
Finally I was fed up
and left both unfinished.

Last Night Your Lost Memory

Last night your lost memory
Came to me
As spring comes quietly upon a wilderness
As a cool breeze
blows gently across desert sands
As a sick man
without reason finds relief.

That Day Is Not So Far, My Love

That day is not so far, my love,
when pain will halt all ways of life
and inner sorrow reach its limit
and yearning eyes will tire of waiting.
My eyes, my tears will all be taken
my youth, my dreams all lost.
You might, my love, think of my love
and make your frail heart sad;
you might come shedding tears upon my grave
and place a few spring flowers on the dust.

You might, my love, just walk over my grave,
laugh at my senseless devotion
(You will not think much of all this
but my broken heart will soldier on),

You may laugh when all is over
You may cry and weep and scream
You may regret the past, or be glad of it –

Your lover will be asleep, uncaring.

Loneliness

Has anyone come again, sad heart?
No, there is no-one there.
A wayfarer perhaps?
He'll go elsewhere.

The night has melted into nothingness,
the dim twinkling of stars
has disappeared.
The sleepy lamp falters in the hallway;
the street has fallen asleep,
giving up on travellers.
Alien dust
has wiped out all the footprints.
Blow out the lamps,
take away the wine, the glass and bottle.
Lock your dreamless doors!
No-one will come here now
no-one
no more.

I Search Again for a Word Today

1
I search again for a word today
a soulful word, a hurtful word
a gentle word, an angry word
A word of love like a lover's glance
which meets me like a kiss,
so bright like a golden wave
like the advent of song
upon a gathering of friends
A word of hatred, like an awesome sword
which destroys forever the tyrant's city,
so dark a word like blackest night
so black that when I speak it
my lips are blackened.

2
Every melody, every note dislocated
the singer's voice searches her being;
like the rent garment of Majnoon*
every string is broken with this pain.
The people beg the breeze to bring
some song, some voices
even an elegy would do
even a sad song would do
even the sound of judgment day
even the scream that heralds
the world's destruction.

* Majnoon literally means 'possessed' or 'mad', and refers to
the powerful Arabic story of Qais's love for Leila. Qais was obsessed to
the point of madness and sacrificed everything for his love. In both
Persian and Urdu poetry, the tale exalts the power and moral value of
love.

Prayer

Come let us also raise our hands to pray,
we who have forgotten how,
we who know no god, no idol,
only love. Come, let us ask life
To infuse the sweetness of tomorrow
in the bitter gloom of today,
To lessen the burden of days and nights
for those who have no strength to bear it,
To light a lamp in the darkness
of eyes that cannot hope to see
the face of dawn.

Come let us ask life
To show a way out to those who are lost
on endless streets;
To give the courage of heresy and the desire for truth
to those who follow the religion of lies and hypocrisy;
To give strength to those whose heads are bowed in fear,
so they can break the murderer's grip.

Love's hidden secret is the fevered soul.
Let us make a pact and slake this fever.
Let us accept the true word
throbbing in our hearts.
So that our anguish is over,
so that our hearts are mended.

N.M.RASHED

1910–75:

Born in Gujranwala, West Punjab, N.M.Rashed is considered by many to be the leading 'modernist' poet in Urdu. A controversial figure, he was highly respected by both friends and opponents; he was fiercely intellectual, anti-populist and anti-propagandist. Rashed wrote long poems mainly in free verse; he published many volumes, edited several magazines and worked for radio and for the United Nations.

Speak

Speak to me,
show me what my face looks like
burnt by the fire of your eyes.

Speak to me,
remove the veil from my face
on which the rainbow of lies has settled,
the hopeless, worn-out rainbow.
Yesterday you saw how
I, a beggar, was found
frozen, outside the morning's wall.
Your eyes kept searching, staring;
but how could I believe in their warmth?
I was lost in the abyss of my own sorrows
and broken memories.

Speak to me,
there is no distance now
between this night and dawn.
Speak to me
so your speech is engraved
on death's face.
Sink now
into my eyes, my ears, my lips
and set alight the flame of language
on the streets of desolate cities.
Let the waves of mystery
ripple across the air.

Pledge

Do not doubt my love,
for my promise is eternal.
The lamp throws a shadow
on the wall, like an arch.
For years that shadow has remained;
so long as the lamp burns, the shadow lives,
its promise eternal.
You are my lamp and I your shadow;
I live so long as you have light –
my promise is eternal.

An insect climbs the wall
fearful of dangers, quivering,
knowing only the limit of the shadow
as the limit of its world.
Yes, my wishes are no more than that
but don't despair of love –
my promise is eternal.

Yes, my promise is eternal.
Life is not just sand and sun
for the crocodiles;
though lying on the sand
they keep a deep attachment to the depths
they came from, drunk with desire.
There is a certain pleasure in the sand.
I too am drunk like a crocodile,
with desire and its whims,
and feel helpless as I lie.
I too am restless,
yearning for love,
lusting after pleasure;
and instead of your devotion
I seek your body's warm embrace.

But do not look at my desire
with disdain,
do not lose faith in my love –
for my promise is eternal.

The Eyes of Dark Sorrow

How they glimmer in the dark,
the eyes of black sorrow —
as if he came disguised as a tyrant
or the new dictator!
A spider has blocked all ears with cobwebs,
lips are locked and sealed
and every heart is pierced.

In the dark
even the dirty teeth of sorrow gleam
just as
through the back door, a tyrant enters
a man's home.
And like a tyrant, sorrow is a meteor
or a ball of flame
killing all in its path.

Sorrow thundered and rained
like a tyrant thunders and rains.
The villagers huddled from a vague fear,
then came out on to the streets.
O God! they cried, O Creator!
How long will the shadow of sorrow
weigh on us?
When will the orders be given?

Revenge

I do not remember her face or features.
All I recall is a bedroom,
a naked body near the fireplace,
on the floor a carpet,
on the carpet a bed,
and in the nooks and corners of the walls
idols of stone and bronze
laughing and sneering!
And in the fireplace the crackle of coals,
angry at the paralytic idols.
The shadow on the high white walls
remembrance of those foreign rulers
whose swords laid the foundations
of white rule here.

I do not remember her face or features
but her naked body I do recall –
a stranger's body
from which my lips had tasted revenge
for the helpless people of my country.
Yes, I remember that naked body.

My Insect Soul

My insect soul
my wretched ant-like soul
kept crawling, nightlong
at the foot of walls,
making snaky patterns.

When she opened the door
I was found dead
(but my dreams lived on).

I have always hated pity.
Friends, you never thought
that from this loss I wrought
the unity of word and meaning
(for which my insect soul kept crawling,
making snaky patterns).
Little did you think
that my dreams,
which lie like dust over my death
and which you will hide for centuries
in holy places,
will tear the camphor shroud of love,
emerge suddenly out of woolly clouds of faith
and become the cure for many ills, ages hence,
in museums.
Did you not fear that?

They laughed at me
as if I stole these thoughts
from their hearts, and said:
Yes, there is a danger of that.
Come, let us burn this dead one
once again
(but make sure to destroy also his dreams).
Let us allow him to crawl
let him crawl for years

so that no dreams are born in his eyes
let him crawl
let him crawl for years
and save the future generations
from the sorrow of consciousness.

The Dust Is Upon Us

The dust has settled on the walls,
it covers all the doors,
it crawls on the red-tiled roofs,
it peeps through blue windows.
Stop all your games!
Fill the cracks in the windows,
the holes in the doors,
with the golden playing-cards!
Stop! Stop! Dust,
you have swallowed those nights,
those slow drizzles
that were not so difficult to catch and chew.
We laughed all night, dust
you were a maddened cat
running after its tail
while night kept licking things away.
Dust has a lifetime, an age;
but it cuts us off from ourselves, this dust,
the way it tries to smother us,
becoming like our death,
giving life to long-forgotten memories.
We pick up sand in our hand
and watch it trickle through our fingers
and slide over our limbs;
our tears seep into it and disappear,
it gets entangled in our hair,
fills our clothes,
lacerates our lungs,
spreads all over us,
in our bodies,
within our souls;
it encompasses us,
this dust.
Dust was a stark denial,
dust was once a boundary;
dust was the synonym

for the pain of knowing.
It was our search.
We were everything and everyone
in dust
alone, solitary.
Dust was that territory
on which no enemy could tread,
which no one could possess.

Today we hear
that senility and loneliness
arrive on dust and leave
the mark of night on day's shoes.
Dust has brought
limitless amazement;
it has stormed
the desolation of our hearts.

The Hand of Music

This hand of music that emerged
from the silence where our voices lay submerged –
the music of this hand
will be the inspiration
of new cities, cultures, societies.
This hand is not a stolen piece
from a bronze idol,
it is a hand soaked in history.
It is not the hand of powerful God;
it is not a beggar prophet's hand.

See,
this hand quivers like a flame,
calling to us: 'Come,
pick the scattered leaves from the roads
and write.'
It says 'Come,
let me show you new dreams
of new halls, new gardens,
lamps, districts, monuments.
These isolated flowers, alien to their kind
in deserts, alone, panting –
let us pile them high in new lawns.
Those confused moments, enveloped
by walls of thought
will be our garland,
will enter our breasts and give birth to mad hopes.'
It says:
'This hand is my daily bread;
this beckons me to live.'
Let's lift a glass of wine with this hand;
let's open the window to the sun's rays
and pray; let's worship the fragrance
brought to us this day.
It says:
'On pity's doorstep

52

lies an ageing love
from whose dried face
let's erase
the tears with this very hand.'
This hand
is a fragment of the sun.
Let's bow to this hand as supplicants;
for in life and death's
every sunlight, every shade,
it will be the consummation
of word and meaning,
the inspiration of every kiss
and all our dreaming.

Dance

Partner, hold me tight!
I have come to you as one escaped from life;
I tremble lest life walk in
through the back door of this dance-hall
to find me committing the crime of joy.

Partner, hold me tight –
The steps of this dance
are like a vague intoxicant.
Look how eagerly I trample sorrow!
I say this to myself:
Before life looks into this dance-hall
I shall crush each single pebble of pain.

Partner, hold me tight
for life is no less than a hungry wolf
in search of me.
Beautiful stranger, each moment
I draw closer to you from fear of this life.
I know you mean not much to me
and we may never meet again;
yet you are those dreams and yearnings
that have always strayed from me.

Partner, hold me tight;
I am not a man of this fragmented age,
I am a slave in this place,
my dreams and wishes colourless, exhausted;
but, if I cannot snatch and pounce on life
at least, here, I can embrace you.
So hold me close,
O stranger, beautiful woman
hold me tight!

Afraid of Life?

Afraid of life?
You too are life, I too am life!
Afraid of man?
You too are human, I too am human!

Man is tongue, man is speech:
you are not afraid of that!
Man is caught in the grip of word and meaning
and life is linked to man:
You are not afraid of that!
You fear the unsaid,
that moment not yet here; you fear
the coming of the moment, the knowledge
of its coming!

They have passed before,
the ages of despondency, of godlessness;
still you think it vain to hope,
and call this night of silence
the way of God!

But you do not know
that when lips are motionless
the limbs awake
becoming signs on the road,
becoming sounds of light;
hands speak out as morning prayers –
Afraid of light?
You too are light, I too am light!
Afraid of light?

The shadow of evil
that lay over the city
is no longer there;
night's cloak at last is torn,
becoming dust.

From the crowd of people
came the voice of man,
came the voice of self.
As in the way of love,
the traveller's blood races,
madness pounces!
Men emerged,
men laughed, cities were settled –
You are already frightened of now?
You too are now, I too am now!
You are afraid already?

In the Silence of Endless Night

On your soft bed my love
in the silence of endless night
my limbs become drunk with lust
and my mind becomes quicksand
in some wilderness, heavy with pleasure.

Sleep, like a hunted prey
like some frightened bird
flaps its wings and shrieks.
In the silence of endless night
on your soft bed my love
my desires roam the peaks of your breasts
and crawl like beaten slaves.

For a moment then I think
that you are not my love:
you are a maiden of some island
and I an enemy of your country
who is forever seeking
a night to lighten his burden;
who, agitated and anxious,
deserts his friends and comrades
in search of limitless pleasure.
This thought also comes into my heart
on your soft bed my love
in the silence of the night.

MIRAJI

1912–49:

Born in Punjab, his real name was Mohammad Sana'ullah. He is credited with introducing free verse in Urdu poetry. Miraji was controversial both for his style and for his subject-matter, which explored sexual and erotic themes. He was accorded an important place by critics, though he did not win the degree of public acclaim of his contemporaries Rashed, Faiz and Ali Sardar J'afri.

Progress

At each step lies a coffin,
go and raise it to your shoulders.

What are you looking at,
it's not my job,
it's yours, and today's
and tomorrow's task.

You, lost in today,
think that neither yesterday
nor tomorrow belong to you!
But if you think like this
nothing will be done.

Go and pick them up,
those coffins lying there.
Go on!

How long will they flow, these tears?
Rise up and wipe them away!

This is not a road,
it is a grave.
Remember, into the grave
only a coffin will go.
So what?
Are you going to crawl away
from the realm of the senses?

There are coffins lying around.
Go and bury them.

The grave is open
like the gaping mouth of a greedy man
but no!
Not even a stale morsel can enter it,

the open mouth remaining open,
empty space.

Lift them up, quickly,
those coffins lying in your gaze,
Go and bury them!

Go and put them to a deep
eternal sleep in the grave.
When these corpses are buried
maybe you'll wake from the dead.

Waves of Pleasure

I want the world to see me,
see me as
someone sees a delicate branch
a delicate, soft and supple branch

But the weight of leaves
should lie by the bed
like a dress
on the floor, all crumpled

I want the breeze to envelop me
delighted, provoking, laughing,
saying words without meaning,
hesitant with desire, faltering,
I want to walk, to run,
into the colourful arms of pleasure,
like the breeze that, touching and caressing
the waves, passes by
with a whisper

If a bird sings anywhere
I want the warm melodious waves of its song
to crash against my body and rebound
in an unstopping tide

Warm rays, soft breeze,
sweet, magic phrases,
new colours, unseen colours
emerge and dissolve in the air.
Nothing must stagnate
in my realm of pleasure and delight,
embracing me, ever closer.
The open field of corn spreads out;
in the distance the sky's blanket
tempts me with sweet gestures

The sound of water, lapping against the shore
dissolves in birdsong
and slips out of sight

I sit
my scarf fallen from my head
I don't care if a stranger sees my hair
My senses embrace me,
let nothing disturb
this domain of pleasure.

AKHTAR-UL-IMAN

Born in 1915 in Bijnor, Uttar Pradesh, he graduated from the Anglo-Arabic College, Delhi.

Since 1946 he has worked as a song-writer and director in the Bombay film industry. He is one of the leading modernists of Urdu, a socialist, and a member of the Progressive Writers Association.

An Evening with a Black-and-White Feathered Bird*

When day is over and the sun hides behind the earth,
and the beehive buzzing heat of the bazaar
and all its commotion of cars, buses, trams, is over;
when the teenagers take their under-age lovers
from the tea-shops and dance-halls
into secret places
and quiet reigns over the spreading, rising tenements;
when theatres and clubs are locked up for the night
and an apparent sleep descends upon the world,
I sit in my room and contemplate:
Why do dogs have crooked tails?
Why do learned men, philosophers, thinkers
go on writing big fat books
on this speckled world which has no character,
no philosophy, no standards, no lasting values?

Furqat's mother made such a fuss over her husband's death,
but a week before her mourning ended
she landed up in Badayun, with Neelum's uncle.
What connects these rituals
of candy, holy books, accounts of holy wars,
the life of the prophet, rejection of the world,
and the sweet tooth of the mullah?

Days are uprooted;
they are black-feathered gulls
that disappear hiding these moments
of laughter and playfulness beneath their wings.
Peace is like a fantasy for those
whose dreams are patched and torn;
they stitch one side and it tears on the other.
This world lives from moment to moment.

* There is no literary allusion intended in any of the characters
named in this poem.

Marium is a seamstress now,
she is losing her sight;
and Gazanfar,
who used to throw sweets tied in a handkerchief
into her house
and write poems in praise of her eyes,
has married elsewhere.
Now he sits in his timber yard
telling tales of wild oats and youth.
Returning home from the shop
he keeps an eye on his daughter –
kids these days are not the same,
sin and sex are on the increase,
how good the old days were!

Sit beneath the Bodhi tree
or go and get crucified,
the bulls will go on fighting.
We have learned to live with death,
a corpse is carried daily on the road;
but what lies behind escapes us all.
In front of us, as always
is a festival of colour, voices, faces.

A bird goes and sits on a branch.
In the pipal tree the parrot has hatched.
The bird we caught yesterday, died.

How many buds have sprouted in Najma's flowerbed?
What do we remember when we smell flowers?
This is an old story: when they first installed street lamps
and I became aware of a heart inside myself,
we had new clothes made for Eid*

* A Muslim holy festival.

and sent sweets to the neighbours.
I sat in the room upstairs
throwing flowers into Zainab's courtyard.
Tomorrow Zainab's house will be auctioned;
it's been in state custody for years.

It seems that autumn has arrived;
I can hear leaves fall incessantly.
Smallpox vaccine stops illness;
contraception and abortion will stop population growth.
When the ape walked on two feet
his brain became active.
The sound of falling leaves is incessant,
there are new faces on the street every day.
We have learned to live with death
but what lies behind escapes us all.
What do we remember when we smell flowers?
When flowers lay rotting near the roundabout
the hanging of the princes was announced.*
This world lives from moment to moment.
The streets of Delhi are the same,
full of life and gaiety.
Days are black-feathered gulls
that hide all moments
beneath their wings and disappear.
Different coloured flags wherever you look.
The cure for human pain and suffering,
the prescription for happiness
lies folded in every pocket.
But why is it that
when we open it,
1957 goes
and 1947 comes?

* The 'hanging of the princes' refers to the aftermath of the
1857 Indian revolt, when the last Moghul princes were executed.

Pride of Cities

How can you hear a scream in this huge city
among the clamouring buses and thundering trains?
There is a buzzing of bees in the constant crowd.
Catch someone and murder him in broad daylight, if you please!
Go rob a woman of her chastity, she's yours!
Who will hear a scream in this vast city?

Big cities, my friend, are for big projects:
speeches of honoured ministers, processions of leaders,
marches, demonstrations, unity and all that.
This is the place for night people, decadence –
whoever told you this was a centre of learning?

Look! just freshly arrived, a royal personage –
and all the important city gents will lick
his boots and present him with a petition;
then after that some president of a bank,
some new ambassador, some new leader,
some manager with plans for industry,
a delegation for cultural exchange,
big plans, big sacrifices, big talk,
functions, parties, big hotels, big big tricks –
Big cities, gentlemen, are for big people.

But there are those in here who are nameless;
came to laugh at the golden city
but they had a long way to go,
those who came to build this world.
They all had big hearts, big souls,
were full of knowledge, wit,
but in the politics of the world were small.
A big city is for big works my friend!

A breaking heart is not a rocket that you can see;
in a big city, who can hear a scream?

Wild Grass

No date of birth, nor place, background unknown.
Where has he come from? Fatherless
he was brought and admitted
to the local charity hospital.
The patient screams at night:
'I have a wounded bird inside me!
Take it out! It's choking, breathless, frightened,
oppressed, afflicted, save it, please!'
The patient screams, groans in agony;
he shouts, and sometimes mutters:
'Vietnam! Dominican . . .' sometimes 'Kashmir,
mineral wealth, dark races, raw material,
crude oil, people, exploitation . . .
the death of the world, air battles, cruelty,
hegemony, pretty women, children, music and song . . .
literature, poetry, peace, destruction;
the funeral of love, sound of drums, dead thought;
progress, cradles of knowledge, coffins of souls,
God's execution, the groaning stars forlorn . . .'
All night he utters unconnected phrases.
The patient has become a cause of great concern.
A storm of complaints from everywhere,
they had to pack him off to another hospital.
It's heard that there, psychiatrists,
consultants and experts have been called.
And all agree
that it is some mental illness.
'The patient must have had a pet bird
which died due to lack of care
resulting in the patient's sorry state.
It's very strange indeed, man's subconscious.
It's nothing but a feeling of guilt
that's captured the patient's mind.
He feels himself a murderer and a criminal.'
Some say,

'The patient is a person belonging to a backward race,
hence dark races have become taboo for the poor man.'
Others speculate that the patient is a patriot
who dreams of self-sufficiency,
who dreams of a free and independent country,
of oil wells discovered in his own land.
There are some who think he is a mere poet
who wants to spend his days wandering around
attracting pretty women, enjoying himself,
achieving fame through his pen, acquiring wealth
in this manner; but the poor man is a failure,
constant lack of success and insecurity
have brought him down.
All faculties collapsed
while speculation continued.
He kept screaming
and no cure was found.
One session after another,
examinations every day and night;
some time was spent thus, and he remained the same.

Then, one evening, she came darkly,
one who was his true doctor.
His agonized screams were never heard again;
the painful music subsided.

It was ages ago, that incident.
The dark embrace has hidden him for ever.
And yet, the walls and doors of the hospital,
where he passed through, still echo:

'Tyrants, do something!
There is a wounded bird inside me!
It's choking, breathless, frightened!
Save it, it is afflicted and oppressed!'

My Friend Abul Haul

The man who just made this fiery speech
builds a bridge of his words,
gives opiate of promises to the young
and takes them to that bridge
and pushing them over it to sink,
returns to his place and relaxes in his armchair.

The world has been carved up by men
who mould sorrow and pain into weapons
or own ordnance factories
or sing in praise of them, while
we have to settle for slogans.
The stylish men who rule the industrial age
may be murderers, or may give life,
but all we can say is
Great! Fantastic! Well done!
He knows well how brave we are,
our courage nothing but chauvinism,
prejudice, communalism, and not much more.
We wrote Alexander's victories
on slates, then rubbed them out, long ago.
Our brave lie in the dust;
their swords hang in museums,
their armour rusty and worn out,
their colourful robes moth-eaten.
He knows well what we are really made of.
Were not our stomachs in our heads
and our genitals on our faces
we would be good men;
all the back doors of our houses lie open.
In our blood there are green, red, yellow flags
but we never hear a word of truth,
our tongue never accompanies our heart.
For us, the empty word democracy and the speeches
that leaders make;
for us, newspaper pages and sexy ads;

for us, idols, religion, the word of God,
colourless like our present,
smelling like raw cloth;
for us only the struggle for bread,
the desire for naked flesh
and nothing more.
The acid in our veins
burns our insides,
goes on burning, burning!

ALI SARDAR J'AFRI

Born in 1912 in Balrampur, Uttar Pradesh, he graduated from the Anglo-Arabic College, Delhi.

A leading intellectual of the left, he was a major figure in the Progressive Writers Association and edited several radical journals, notably **Naya Adab** (New Literature); he was a member of the Communist Party of India and editor of its literary magazine, **Indian Literature**, from Bombay. Sardar J'afri has published several volumes of verse, criticism and prose, and works in film and television.

One Year

1
What is the meaning of imprisonment,
what the significance of jails?
O year now asleep in time's graveyard,
on your shrivelled shadow
barking jaildogs weep.
I look at all this and I laugh.

Those venomous stings of moments past
the blood-soaked sharpness of the morning's sword
that blackness left in the evening's eye
by gunpowder
the infantry of weeks, the cavalry of months
who came to crush my revolt
all those I've left sleeping
by your side O passing year.

Blood drips from the eyes of sentries
the rifles speak through lips of steel
and bullets sting with tongues of brass
and LAW, that chain of property,
extends its links and gathers more
within its deceptive embrace
year after year the snake changes its form
inside the charmer's basket
poisonous cobras lurk, upholding the rule
of LAW and JUSTICE
while his flute hides the hissing
within its waves of melody.

Still the proud hearts of selfless
fighters are beating,
the throb of struggling veins resounds;
and through time and history's streets
pass the processions.

2

How many youthful yearnings bled in China
to adorn the face of the new dawn?
And how many hearts the free beauties of Greece
have sown in anticipation of spring!
The tears that rained down
from the eye of Spain are restless
to become pearls and dewdrops.
Like a bright banner the blood of martyrs
from Vietnam and Malaya
is shimmering in the mirror of the sky.
The Burmese earth has given birth to flames
whence will arise new spring flowers.
The fire of revolt in Tilangana
rushes to burn the fields of slavery.
The wounded spirit of Bengal
has recovered its might.
Pain and cries for mercy
have found the fiery language
of slogans demanding, demanding.
From every quarter the bursting force of floods;
from each atom the dance of emerging light.
Pain of death, terror of slavery
and against them,
WAKING AND RISING HUMANITY!

What is imprisonment?
What is the significance of jails?

3

What are days and nights
but milestones on the roads;
months and years are dust left
by travellers.
Imprisonment comes and passes.
We meet mountains of trouble,

valleys of ignorance
hearts burning in deserts of starvation,
life burns in the boiling river of blood
and in the thorny wastes of bayonets
footsteps become red lines of blood.
Yet the caravan moves towards the destination.
Eyelids unveil the scenery
dreams erupt with flowers.

4
I am not lonely here
for so many yearnings are imprisoned with me:
so many youthful faces bred in mountain valleys
so many sons of the green fields
so many workers who drive trains and machines
so many fragrances from kisses
so many curls of lovely hair
so many sisters' flowers of hope
so many mothers' dreams
so many storms and gales
so many strikers' mutilated hands
so many banners of revolt!

The higher the mountain to climb
the greater the courage we muster.
Our courage is like the Himalayan eagle's flight,
whose beating wings
unleash a snowstorm in the heights!

And the old prisoners, wise friends
whose wrinkles are pages of historical events,
the laughter in their sparkling eyes
the wrinkles of their smiles
are a mockery of the system's cruelty.
In this night of slavery
the silver of their hair foretells

that morning is approaching
and those passionate poets and storytellers
melt the chains of worry
with the warmth of their song.

Each verse tells a story of heroism,
each song shakes these walls!

The flames of voices rise with such force
that they ignite the dark dungeons
and our destination glows in the arch
of time, a ray from the morning sun.
Thousands of suns and moons and stars
immerse my mind in a flood of light.

If I have companions like these
then the purpose of travelling is great!
If the night is so bright
how much brighter the dawn!

Central Jail, Nasik, India, April 1950

Robe of Flame

Who is that
standing in a robe of flame?
body broken, blood spilling
from his brains.

Farhad and *Qais* passed away*
some time ago; who then is he
whom people stone to death?

There is no beautiful *Shireen* here,
no *Leila* of spring seasons.
In whose name, then, this scarlet bed
of wounds is flowering?

It is some madman
stubbornly upholding Truth,
unbending to the winds of lies and cunning.

It is clear, his punishment must be
Death by stoning!

* Qais (Majnoon) and Leila, Farhad (Kohkun) and Shireen
symbolize enduring love in Urdu poetry, love of a kind that is shocking
and disgraceful in the eyes of the orthodox.

The Final Night

Chairs, tables, lamps, chandeliers,
clinking of glasses,
bottles hiding laughter and song
in their long necks.
Colour of wine, appearing in the glasses,
staining them red.

The blood of Korea
in the eyes of Yankee officers,
bodies of young men chopped up
on plates; mothers' breasts
in the claws of sharp forks, babies
under American knives,
barbecued on bomb fires;
the wine of tears, the song of screams.
This is the final night,
the last round, the final drink.
Look, out there, outside the window,
the young Korean night burns like gunpowder!
In the air, like lightning,
the warcries
of Seoul's raiders!

This Blood

What will you do with
this blood
warm as a kiss, red as a rose,
smile of an infant, prayer on an old man's lips,
blackness of seductive eyes, pink of soft hands,
song of the lyre, tune of a poet's heartstring,
love's promise.

This blood is not an infidel, nor an atheist,
nor a Muslim.
The melody of the Vedas and the Gita,
harmony of the holy book, this,
the first compelling word of the book of life,
the very first canto of desire;
the soul of the Bible, the heart of the Torah.
The thirst of knives
cannot be quenched with this flame.

What will you do with
this blood?
so young, so warm, so red.
When spilt on dust, it will sear
the earth's womb.
The heavens will withhold their rain
of blessings.
No seedling will ever throw up shoots,
no buds sprout nor flowers perfume.

This blood, the fragrance of lips,
the light in our eyes.
This blood, the colour of cheeks,
the heart's solace,
the sun that shines on Mount Faran,
the vision on Sinai.
Flame of the True Word,
the burning of restless spirits.

The brightness of Truth,
the manifestation of Light!

This blood, my blood, your blood,
Everyone's blood!

Tears of Shame

Where are the tears of shame
to wash the blood from our clothes
and the dirt of suspicion from our hearts?

Were they here, those tears,
our spirit would find strength.
This Man now caught in hate
and trapped in lust and greed,
victim of his own politics,
this Man would dwell in love,
becoming god.

KAIFI A'ZMI

Born in 1924 in Azamgarh, Uttar Pradesh, his real name is Athar Husain Rizvi.

A member of the Communist Party and a popular revolutionary poet, he was active in the Progressive Writers Association and an editor of **Naya Adab** (New Literature). A'Zmi is renowned as a lyricist in the film world. His poems have been collected in **Jhankar, Akhiri-Shab** and **Awara Sajde.**

Bangladesh

I am not some country which you can destroy.
I am not a wall which you can demolish
Nor a frontier that you can wipe out.

This world map
You have spread upon the table
Has only lines on it.
Why do you search for me in there?
I am the yearning of the possessed.
I am the brutal dream of the oppressed.

When looting reaches its limit
When cruelty breaks all bounds
I suddenly appear
In some corner, in some person.
You must have seen me before,
In the East, in the West,
In cities, in villages,
In towns, in wildernesses.
I have no geography
I dwell only in history
And a history that cannot be taught.
People read it secretly
Because today I could be the victor, tomorrow
The defeated.
Sometimes I hanged the murderer
and often I was hanged.
The only difference is –
My murderers die, I do not
nor can I.
How foolish you are!
The tanks you've got on charity
you drive on to my breast
and rain your napalm day and night.
Look, you'll get tired!
Which hands will you chain?

My hands number seventy million!
Which head will you chop off?
I have seventy million heads!

Stray Prostrations
(on the breakdown of communist unity)

My only wealth is my pain.
Who can I take this offering to?
I see no hangman by the gallows
who will take my heart and soul!
You too are my love, my friend
Yet you are unacquainted, distant,
You too!
You were the cure, the ultimate salvation, you;
Yet you have no cure, not even you.

It is not easy to carry one's own corpse.
My hands grow weak and falter.
Those very followers who stood at our door
are now becoming wanderers, straying.
Our goal was far, yet not so distant
for us to lose our way.
I would not settle for a small wound;
the love of martyrdom drove me to the gallows!

When my legs gave way, exhausted
I knew
I had no one but myself as guide.
One god followed another to rule over me;
I got fed up and said
I have no god!

AHMAD NADEEM QASMI

Born in 1916 in Sargodha, he graduated from Bhawalpur.

A prominent journalist and progressive poet, he is also a renowned short-story writer, famous for his representation of Punjabi culture in his stories. He lives in Pakistan.

Civilized

I met a friend yesterday
who revealed to me this secret:
'The days of love and passion are gone'
he said.

Then, looking around nervously,
he added:
'Roll up your carpet of love,
gather money wherever you can get it.
Listen to me,
become civilized.'

Firing

I agree;
you said when you heard the sound
that bullets had been fired.
But I, in the clamour
of breaking bones and spurting blood
had buried the corpse of my hearing
before I could hear
the sound of firing!

A Bull

You are so thick-skinned!
You get whipped
and just twitch your ears.
Even when it's painful
you refuse to use your horns.
You use your own tail to whip yourself
and shake your head from side to side
when you hear the sound of new whips,
adding to the rhythm
with your shovelling hooves!
When your skin is torn to shreds
you only give out a burp
then die
quietly.

AHMAD FARAZ

Born in 1936 in Kohat, NWFP, Faraz is one of the most popular Urdu poets of today, known wherever Urdu is spoken. He came to prominence as a romantic *gazal* writer, but in recent years has established himself as a modern poet with socialist and progressive themes. He was jailed in Pakistan for his outspoken rejection of military rule, and now lives in exile in Britain. English translations of his work have been published in Canada, and a new volume of translations is expected to be published in England soon.

Preface

It's an old story:
When lips thought of speaking words,
giving them life
in sound
they had to drink
a cup of hemlock.
Rulers feared
that words
given life with voices
might become a story.
And those lips were silenced;
but the quivering, sighing words,
wounded by the killer's sword,
kept throbbing,
voiceless.
Who could have known
that the blood of those words
would drop by drop
become lines that shine?
And now these lines of blood
have in themselves become
a story and a fable.

Prophecy of the Winds

All mothers' lips are stones
and their eyes have scars,
their hearts, anxiety.
The night speaks:
'These sons of yours
were taken in the dark
by armed men;
there is no news of their return.'
'Don't even think of their return,'
the winds were saying
to the frightened lamps.
'Even to the coming of new seasons
you shall see no light.
These mothers will remain stones,
their tears stuck in their throats.
They will not be living,
neither will they die.'

Don't Think

And she
pouring red wine into my glass,
said Don't think so much!
You're in a place now – in this country,
in this city – where you can enjoy yourself,
where everyone is dancing, singing, swinging.
Stop thinking, relax!
What sort of people are you?
Even when you go abroad
you bring your sickly night and day,
your broken heart, your memories of friends,
like your soiled torn shirts
whose stains cannot be cleaned
by the machines of laundries –
these scars of poverty,
this self-destructive darkness of the soul
this self-neglect, you carry them
as if they were dear to you!
But here where you are now,
life is no dream,
nor a whirlpool of thought;
life here is like wine – daring, seductive,
not a poison.
Leave your begging-bowl at the doorstep,
begging is not the done thing here,
relax,
don't think so much!

Crucifixion of the Word

Come, let us mourn
the bloodied corpse of that Jesus
whom we crucified,
and weep.
We have done our duty well;
it is time to settle accounts.

Let him take the slippers
who made the cross;
the shroud belongs to he
who nailed him;
and he deserves the crown of thorns
whose eyes had tears.

Come, let us claim now
we are all Christ;
let us also show them
we can wake the dead!
But his word was everything:
Where is the word?

Mercenaries

For so long I sang your praises
but now I'm ashamed of my songs,
disturbed by the fame of my poems,
ashamed of the way I used my craft.
With guilt I look at imprisoned friends,
with shame I look at those I love.

Whenever on my beloved soil swooped
an enemy or the shadow of oppression,
whenever murderers came to attack,
whenever aggressors crossed the border
I gave whatever I had,
blood and my craft to serve you.

With tears we said goodbye to you
when battle called you away;
little hope was there of victory, though
even in defeat we never let you out of our hearts.
You sold your dignity to preserve your life;
still we tolerated your treachery.

The oppressed of the East were ours too,
whose blood you wiped on your face.
Did you really go to crush revolt
or did you go to plunder and rape?
How could you change their fate? –
You were too busy trying to wipe them out!

Whatever the outcome, let's say
the night of troubled dreams was over.
With such vanity you went there,
with such humiliation you left, for prison!
You went with pomp and splendour of arms,
with chains around your necks you left.

Still I said you were not to blame,
just to please the people of the city.
Though my poems were no balm for your wounds
still, just to comfort the helpless,
for my lost landscape
for my hopeless, sad people, I sang.

You may remember too those days
when from prison you returned.
Broken-hearted we lined the streets,
tears in our eyes,
forgetting the bitterness of our humiliation
we showered you with flowers of pride.

Little did we know that you, the defeated
would come to lick our open wounds,
that you who knew the taste of blood
would break all bounds of cruelty,
that after the killing in Bengal
you'd come and slaughter in Bolan.

Why have you put up gallows
in Frontier, in Punjab and Mehran?
Heroes!
Why and for whom this butchery,
before whom are you humble, heroes!
Which tyrant has ordered you to this,
for whom, heroes! do you shed this blood?

Little did I know that you would bring
such dark night on our land.
Yesterday you waved the flag of tyranny
and today you crawl in the tyrant's court.
For one dictator's sake you hold a sword
against so many necks.

Like the Gurkhas under the British,
brutal and bestial,
like the white mercenaries in Vietnam
who also accused the freedom fighters, –
You are no different; they too had
rifles, uniforms, names.

You have seen the processions of people,
banners of revolt in their hands.
The drying blood on the pavements
signifies that judgment day is near.
Yesterday we had only love for you
but today the flames of hate are rising in our hearts.

Today even the poet must perform his duty;
in the pen there's blood, not ink.
When your mask came off, then we knew
that you are not soldiers, but hired killers.
It's no longer just the tyrant's head we want,
we demand the blood of all collaborators!

Demon

Frightened mothers
hold infants to their breasts
and shudder.
For years,
villagers claim,
there's been a demon
in this area
who has many faces
and whenever
in any home
the lamp of voices is lighted
or the flower of hope blooms
he comes
and eats up everyone
before daybreak.

Many times
so many good men
sorrow's embers
in their breasts
and their wounded eyes
full of stars
went out to hunt this demon
only to be found
next evening
on the twisting, turning path
which leads to the jungle
of black snakes and yellow thorns
their heads
their limbs
their eyes
scattered, blood-spattered pieces.

And seeing this
the villagers have to this day
covered their mouths, their eyes
with their own hands.

Vietnam

I am certain,
when into history's court
time brings today's
bold and cynical murderer,
clothes and sleeves soaked
in the blood of his sins,
all human beings will spit on his face
in hatred and disgust.
But I am also certain of this:
tomorrow, history will also ask us all,
'Yesterday, when in front of you
this same murderer was killing
innocent people of your tribe,
you watched him, spectators,
silent, unmoving
participants in cruelty.
Why were you silent then,
where was your hatred and disgust,
tell me what difference was there
between the murderer's sword
and your arrows of compromise?'
Then I think,
What shall we say?

Beirut

Whose headless body is this
whose scarlet shroud
whose torn and wounded cloak
whose broken voice?

Whose blood is this
that turns the earth a ruby colour,
whose cruel embrace
taking the coffin's shape?

Who are these youths
standing in the line of fire,
what city are they from?

Who are these helpless ones
lying scattered
like a harvest reaped
by enemy swords?

Whose faces have we here,
drops of blood like pearls
glistening on their lips and eyes?

Who is this mother
searching in the debris
for her child,
who is this father
his voice lost
in the terrible chaos?

Who are these innocent ones
extinguished
like lamps
by the dark storm?

Which tribe are they from,
these brave people
ready to die?
No one wants to know them
for knowing them
is like a test;
we see no child, no mother,
no father in their midst.

In the palaces
the lucky sheikhs are silent;
kings are silent,
protectors of the faith,
rulers of the world,
all silent.
All these hypocrites
who take God's name
are silent!

Why Should We Sell Our Dreams?

We may be humble in our ways,
but when were we so poor
as to sell our dreams at your door?

We carried our wounds within our eyes,
but when were we so weak
as to display them on the street?

Our hands were empty
yet we were not so short of pride
as to peddle our dreams in public,
wearing tattered clothes, crying
Dreams for sale! Buy a dream!

Why should we sell our dreams,
dreams for which we gave our eyes,
dreams that were so dear to us
that we gave up all other desires?

True, we are unheard, voiceless,
bereft of honour or fortune;
true, we may be luckless, talentless,
but why should we sell
our fables, the stars and moons
that we have dreamt upon this earth?

Merchants!
You have brought your piles of paper money
from the markets of greed,
you've brought gold and silver coins;
so often you have brought temptation.
But why should we sell to you
the beauty of our word,
the treasure of our blood?

Our dreams may be trifling
and have no meaning
yet they are the dreams of the aggrieved,
they are not the dreams of Zulekha*
putting blame on the Joseph of her desire,
nor the dreams of some Egyptian king,
for his prisoners to interpret;
these are not the dreams of tyrants
who bring helpless men to the gallows
nor the dreams of plunderers
who put the dreams of others to the sword.

Our dreams are the dreams of the pure in heart,
dreams of word and music,
dreams of doors that wait to be opened,
dreams of voices that are silenced.

* Wife of the Egyptian noble in whose house Joseph was
employed in his exile, who, incensed by Joseph's rejection of her, had
him imprisoned on a false accusation.

SAQI FAROOQI

Born in 1936 in India, he now lives in Britain.

A writer of fluent free verse who is violently opposed to traditional imagery, he has published several volumes of poetry; he is also considered an important critic, often making enemies because of his iconoclastic views. As a leading modernist poet, he considers Rashed his mentor. Saqi Farooqi also writes in English.

Morning Sounds

Burrowing into my dreams
the alarm clock's
harsh, hard ring
fell like dew
wetting each petal
on the flower of sleep.

The sleeper
slowly, very slowly
removed the silken curtains
from his eyes
and like the sunflower
turned his gaze towards that
dazzling window
where the broken white feathers
of sunlight
waved and shuddered
in the strong breeze.

A Dog Poem

My dear
for seven years
you have sat
on the television
like the patient, humble dog
of His Master's Voice
unconcerned, content, unaware.

Under your paws
a storm is raging;
living, warm blood
gushes from the television's veins,
spurting out.
The carpet's soaking,
the sofa is afloat,
I drown in my blood!
Help me!
Why don't you bark,
stupid dog!

Spider

Seeing him in my bathtub
I knew that my guest
hid a poem in him.

I took an insect
from the lampshade
and tempted him from afar.
His suspicious eyes
showed no lustre of greed.
He turned his legs upon himself
and sat down as if nothing
had happened.

I thought of a trick.
On a piece of string I made a knot,
then left some space, then another and another . . .
Making a ladder,
I dropped it into the tub.
He, pretending death, in whom a poem of mine lay,
in his cunning quiet way
suddenly came alive
and leapt up the ladder
and scurried away somewhere.

He has run away somewhere
and does not know
that I, too, languish
in the prison tub.
No insect comes my way;
no ladder
can I see anywhere.

Sher Imdad Ali's Tadpole

but
there was
in that murky dim pond
such an air
on the half-blossomed lotus
that it filled his eyes
with rainbow colours

then of course
there was
the inviting, seductive water
giving in to its magical pull
throwing off his clothes
he plunged into the stagnant water
and
got entangled in weeds.

millions of tadpoles
like soft raw headed foetuses
rushed in all directions
frightened by the clamour
of shark waves
Sher Imdad Ali
was in the water
up to his chin
the lotus of his desire
still far away

lightning flashed
and a tadpole
with the speed of a deflating balloon
slipping out of someone's hand
like the dagger tongue of a lizard
whizzed into the tunnel
of his gaping mouth

days passed
seasons changed years went by

a voice keeps hounding him
LET ME OUT
LET ME OUT OF THIS DUNGEON

dozens of doctors surgeons
X-rays were to no avail
he changed homes cities countries
all without relief
in his blood
the same voice
ripples and tosses
LET ME OUT
LET ME OUT OF THIS DUNGEON

Sher Imdad Ali
his stolen property
taken from the water
hides in his house in fear

outside
the water lurks
and in it
like yellow pipal leaves
yellow frogs
angry bastards
lie in wait

Yearning for the Shore

Moonstruck
I
bereft of everything
caught in the fish hook
of moonbeam
motionless, like a dead wave,
lie on the water's surface
numb and half-afloat.

Let the wind blow
so I can receive
the shore's kisses.

Alchemy
(Artificial insemination)

In the veins of glass,
a spark of urgency.
The test tube is alive.
She hears the pounding
of a foreign heartbeat.

From the hooked thorn
of this magical rose
hanging corpselike
the crystal tear of dew
which the anxious ray of hope
cuts with its sharp edge
in her womb.

Daily
from the wound below her navel,
on her yearning body,
fragrances will emerge,
colours flow.

Today,
inside her
the fertility of mothering shell
turns dust to pearl.

The luminous ward,
two bright, white gloves
and a shining pearl.

MUNIR NIAZI

Born in 1928 in Hushiarpur, India, he is a prominent modern poet, imagist in style.

He also writes in Punjabi. Munir Niazi has written many film songs and uses everyday conversational language, avoiding literary diction.

Song of the Wind

Do not hinder my path.
I am the wind.
If you go to search for me
in gardens, mountains, old houses
you will find only pain
and nothing else.
You, who wake up
in dark black nights
at the slightest sound
and glare all around
with burning eyes –
Is there any amongst you
who can take in his arms
running streams, or wayward screams,
who can call back
those who have gone?

A Half-Open Window at Midnight

Half the face illumined
half behind a dark curtain
One eye shines like the sun
the other behind a black veil
The secret is not yet revealed
from the half-fallen mask
The eye as always trapped
between the apparent and the hidden mirage

Let Us Leave Something Unsaid

Let some things remain unsaid.
Let some things remain unheard.
If you say everything that's in your heart
then what will remain inside?
If you have heard every word of the heart
then what will remain to be heard?

Leave a certain
hidden awkwardness.
Leave an unopened window
on the colourful
unmade world.

Rain, Wind and a New City

Rain was on the walls
and roofs
and the dark forest of houses.
The wind was sharp
on faces, doors
and the empty, desolate streets.
Lights
there were, in some places
in the shrines or in the cold
and high buildings.
Maybe he* is also there, somewhere,
in the wilderness
or in the marble mansions.

* The masculine 'he' could be either he, she or He (meaning God).

A Night at a Port

Lights, lights
and the lament of tired ships.
In the rain,
the magic moments of opening doors
showed my heart
the game of days gone by
but it was not impressed.
The city is like a stone;
it is my enemy and thirsts also
for the dancer's blood.
I am lost in thought
and so is the dancer at the hotel,
dancing like one possessed.

Two White Women in the Sun

There it was,
the temple of Durga
There it was
the wind on the road
The sun was a silver mirror
that dazzled the eyes.

A Vague Dream

The taut bow
of the new moon
and the fragrance
surrounding us
the enticing poison
of deep dark colours
a tree, a snake
I and you

A New Colour in the Colour of Sunlight

The yellow flower is a yellow well
in which the bee searches for something
it left behind.
Was it a drop of honey or poison
or a flower petal?
The yellow flower is so bright,
like a lamp turned on
in the sunlight!

MUSTAFA ZAIDI

1930–70:
Before his tragic death, he was considered one of the most promising poets of the younger generation in Pakistan, writing in the romantic/revolutionary tradition of his mentor, Josh Malihabadi.

Renewal

1
Life!
I came to your door like a beggar.
I spread my arms like a begging bowl
in every path you tread.

Not a single shaft of light I got
to wake a dead ray of hope.
The sinking, falling satellite
received no signal from central control.

With a sudden loud blast
the rope slipped out of my hands.
The fingers of hope were blistered,
all the nerves exploded and were torn.

And then the dark silence
the dark hair of dead traditions
some comforting words to keep me going
some old crocodile tears.

2
The lights were drowned in fog
time like fortune was unfriendly
night's face was scarred
like my wounded tolerance.

I went with a desire to do battle
with you
at the edge of a dangerous stream;
I taught the waves to be angry
I initiated the torrents.

When you came, though,
there were no sighs, no anger;
on your face, my tears,
around my neck, your arms!

122

Vietnam

Yesterday, the laughing blue eyes
of my friend
doubted the peril of each new message,
thinking that the face seen in the camp
mirror would return smiling to his home
where someone would kiss him with wet eyes
and would wipe out
possible darkness with a smile.

Today I stand alone,
my cigarette scorching the air,
a mug of tasteless coffee in my hand,
looking at the army blanket
laid out on the stretcher
(his lifeless body's sole companion).
Soon, a coffin-like plane will leave me on the runway
with this final vision.
Then Saigon, in the silence of its airport
will ask of me the same few questions
it asked of someone else.

Madhouse

Spectators lurk everywhere
to see me tear my clothes
and from all directions
emerge horrible faces
of desolation, expectant,
looking for a laugh.

To enjoy a few exciting moments
sane people, with a smile,
have come a long way to watch
and be entertained by tears.

Reason hates everything abnormal.
In the homes of the rational
prophets are not even offered a bench
or stool, let alone a crown or throne.

Our group is one of broken men.
Were we the majority of the world
then they would understand
that the crowd that's gathered
on the other side of the cage
is mad.

SAHIR LUDHIANVI

1921–80:

Born in Ludhiana, East Punjab, his real name was Abd-al-Haye. He was active in student politics, wrote lyrics for many films, and was author of several immensely popular songs. Greatly influenced by Faiz Ahmad Faiz, he wrote mainly progressive and agitational poetry; he received the Lenin Prize, and was active in the Progressive Writers Association.

A Gift of Blood

Searching for a garden in my world
you will find fiery winds, not spring.
No rainbow colours here, in this grey afternoon;
from one end to the other swings the noose.
Once again they go toward their gory end,
those leaders who have lost their way so many times!

Behind the veil of their democracy
they build prisons, they make whips.
In the name of peace they conjure wars,
in the clamour for justice they produce disparity.
Fear guards the heart and lips are sealed;
overhead, the tents of iron bars stretch out.

Yet, have they ever feared cruelty and oppression,
those ideas that have given strength to the imagination?
No mercenary army can ever break the glass
that holds the people's wakened spirit.
At each step, life gives a gift of blood
to the lamps that grapple with the darkness.

Onward moves the caravan of human progress,
shaking the hearts of tyrants.
All around the drums of revolt are sounding,
young people walk about like lighted flames!
The whole earth is a boiling ocean,
The mountains and forests are alive!

It's easy to stifle my scream
but who will stop the challenge of life?
The wall of steel and fire may be high
but who will stop the force of changing times?
You who block the way of new ideas –
Who will stop the sword of mass uprising?

From the very place of darkness where you seek refuge
the armies of morning will emerge!
In the air unfurl the red flags,
East and West converge!

Before Suicide

This wailing in the wind, this heartless dark –
Who knows if there's a morning to this night?
One last look at the open window –
There may not be the strength in my sinking eyes.

They're still burning, the lamps in your room.
Through thin curtains filters the warmth
of some stranger's embrace,
your hair falling darkly across the room.

In the waning light of my candle
emerge dark shadows, arms outstretched.
Who will wipe these burning tears,
who untie these tangled dreams?

Ah, this cave of dying, this half-light,
my life spent within these dim walls!
Life! that heartless whim of nature,
real but spent in dreams.

So many comforts laughed in mansions
as the doors closed on my youth.
So many hands wove silk
but on my body there were rags!

In this cruel and hostile prison
how long can I please myself with dreams?
A day or two of suffering one can bear
but not this life of endless crawling.

The same darkness clouds the horizon.
Who knows when we will breathe freely?
Who knows when the chains will break,
when oppressed humanity will find relief?

They're still burning, the lamps in your room.
Today I will go down into the caves of death;
and with the smoke of the dying candle
I will pass the frontiers of this continuous dying.

Market Place

Those poems that once I wrote for you
I've brought today into the market place.
Today they'll go to the highest bidder,
the songs through which our love found meaning.
Everything is measured now on silver scales,
my thoughts, my poetry, my emotions.
Poverty has turned to commodity
the songs that were as priceless as our love.
Hunger demands a few crumbs and necessities,
instead of the blossoming image of your face.
Look, in this age of capital and labour
my songs are not my own.
You may belong to someone rich;
your pictures cannot remain with me.
Those poems that once I wrote for you
I've brought today into the market place!

Foreign Agents

Tough strong men from foreign lands
stand in front of the VIP door of the tall hotel.
And below, the helpless streets of my helpless country
in which roam aimlessly crowds of hungry men,
hopelessness on their faces
and years of slavery in their blood,
devoid of the light of knowledge, destitute,
the stars, the worn-out stars of the Indian sky
whose thoughts could not reach near
the foot of that mountain on which stand
the tough, strong men from foreign lands,
cigarettes between their lips,
glasses of brandy in their hands,
in their pockets the jingle of silver coins
which buy at night some starving peasant's treasure:
some destitute girl
some helpless girl's vain beauty.
In these hallways resounding with pleasure,
in the bedrooms of the high hotel,
laughing, joking, stand erect
these tough, strong men from foreign lands.

And near this hotel
groups of helpless poor slaves
stare endlessly up at them,
waiting for that precious moment
when the tip of a boot of one of these
carefree foreigners will send down to them
a coin, a cigarette, a piece of cake
or a half-eaten slice of bread,
just to enjoy watching the crowd scramble
and fight each other for it,
to laugh at these dogs!
Groups of hungry helpless slaves stare upwards,
standing silently.
If only these hopeless dejected creatures

131

had strength to change their circumstances,
if only these chained dogs could break their chains
and bite their masters,
if only they stood for each other, helped each other,
if only they had some sense of national pride,
we would not need these hired thugs
to protect us from some vague danger from the east.

Bengal

You philosophers of the old world,
the problems of a new world call to you!
Were these huge boulevards built for this,
so the people can roam upon them homeless?
Did the generous earth give up its treasures
so we could watch the starving die a slow death?
Do our mills weave silk in huge quantity
so the daughters of our land can yearn for thread?
Did the gardener water the plants with his own blood
to wait for the spring that will never come?
Gods of power, managers of factories,
dignitaries of the state!

Five million soiled, broken bodies
are agitating against the system of property.
With silent faces, with dying eyes
man agitates against man.

KISHWAR NAHEED

Born in 1940 at Bulundshehr, she was educated at Punjab University.

Journalist and translator, and Director of Lahore Arts Council, she is considered the leading woman poet in Urdu; her book of poems, **Streets, Sunshine and Doors**, won wide acclaim. Kishwar Naheed writes in free verse and has translated poets such as Pablo Neruda into Urdu. She lives in Pakistan.

Agreement

He says
that I am like a rock
in my coldheartedness.
I think to myself:
How can anyone call this
desire and secrecy cold?
Yes, I have put stones
in my throat.
My sighs hit these stones,
sink back in my body
and erupt in my nerves;
anxiety is burning me.
I never let these flames reach
my eyes or lips;
the stones in my throat
are a wall against my feelings.
On the radar of your mind
you cannot hear the bleeps
of these intruders.

I Am Not That Woman

I am not that woman
selling you socks and shoes!
Remember me, I am the one you hid
in your walls of stone, while you roamed
free as the breeze, not knowing
that my voice cannot be smothered by stones.

I am the one you crushed
with the weight of custom and tradition
not knowing
that light cannot be hidden in darkness.
Remember me,
I am the one in whose lap
you picked flowers
and planted thorns and embers
not knowing
that chains cannot smother my fragrance.

I am the woman
whom you bought and sold
in the name of my own chastity
not knowing
that I can walk on water
when I am drowning.

I am the one you married off
to get rid of a burden
not knowing
that a nation of captive minds
cannot be free.

I am the commodity you traded in,
my chastity, my motherhood, my loyalty.
Now it is time for me to flower free.
The woman on that poster,
half-naked, selling socks and shoes –
No, no, I am not that woman!

Listen To Me

If you want to speak
your punishment is death.
If you want to breathe
your place is in the prison.
If you want to walk
then cut off your legs
and carry them in your arms.
If you want to laugh
hang upside down in a well.
If you want to think
then shut all the doors
and throw away the key.
If you want to cry
then sink into the river.
If you want to live
then become a cobweb on the cave
of your dreams.
And if you want to forget everything
then pause and think:
of the word you first learnt.

Speech Number Twenty-Seven

My voice is the voice of my city.
My voice is the voice of my age.
My voice will influence generations.
What do you think it is,
that you call my voice a clamour?
How can you call my voice
the voice of madness?
How can you think
the coming storm a mere illusion?

I am no prophet,
I only see today with open eyes.
Your barbaric acts
diffused like the stink of money,
you recline in the back seat
of your limousine
so that the harsh sunlight of poverty
will not destroy the surgical creation
that is your face.
Now you can remember each speech
by its number:
Speech number 10, To arouse the poor
Speech number 15, To create consciousness amongst women
Speech number 27, To advise the writers and intellectuals.

Voices, voices, voices –
What is a clamour?
A crescendo of conflicting sounds,
or waves of unconnected speeches?
Stones rolling down the hillside –
Throw a stone in a desert
and it sinks noiselessly in the sand.
But my voice is not a stone,
it is lightning;
after its flash everyone can hear the thunder.
Putting your hands to your ears
will not stop the storm.

Why should those who read about the weather
and make speeches
come to see the flowing gutters in the alleys?
Sowing a little seed of revolution
in its season
will not create a forest of revolution.
You can buy red colour cheaply
but scarves stained with the red of blood
are not so easily bought.

If I am aware of all this,
why aren't you?
I speak the truth.
I am no prophet,
I only see today with open eyes.
That is all.

How Crazy Are Those Who Love You So Much

With words of chastity he adorned my hands,
chained my feet like prisoners,
and called it modesty.
How sweet and pleasant it sounds,
like a diamond,
like the gleam of a knife!
He says: 'What more can you ask for?
Walls of marble, clean and shining
to keep you safe. The gold lock and chain
on big, solid black mahogany doors
at least show that it's all for you,
for your security, for your love.'

How lovingly and hopefully built,
this home full of ideals and dreams!
It's been tested with screams,
making sure that if a sound
dare penetrate some crevice
it will turn to foam, exhausted,
and nothing will get through.

'Tenderly, for you, for your love
this home, this throne, these marble walls.
All for you, my dear,
all because I love you!'

HABIB JALIB

Born in 1929, Jalib is one of the most popular poets in Pakistan, particularly among students.

He writes in very simple language, accessible to the man in the street. A truly political poet, he believes in putting politics above art and uses his verse to arouse the people to fight against oppression. Though conveying modern themes, Jalib seldom uses free verse; he does not defend himself against charges of writing propaganda and slogans, and claims to be a poet of the moment.

On the Banning of a Book of Poems

In my hand I hold a pen,
in my heart the light of consciousness.
How can your forces of oppression
ever win?
I, concerned with peace for all mankind
and you just out to save your precious skin.
Into the world I dawn, the rising sun;
into the ocean of oblivion you shall sink!

My Daughter

Thinking that it was a toy,
when she saw the chain around my wrists
my daughter jumped for joy.

Her laughter was the gift of morning,
her laughter gave me endless strength.
A living hint of a free tomorrow
gave meaning to my night of sorrow.

AMIQ HANAFI

Born in 1928, his real name is Abdul Aziz Hanafi; he lives in India.

Hanafi studied politics and history, and worked as a script-writer and programme executive in All India Radio. He writes in Hindi and Urdu, and has published several volumes of verse.

Poems Are Cheap

In today's expensive atmosphere
poetry is cheap, they say.
Go on reading, poems are cheap.
As on a bright boulevard, a wayward
meaningless evening
As the quarrel over places in a queue
Like swearing
Like slogans
Like womanly anger
Like vomit
Like a cancer wrapped in yellow
Like death.
Poetry is cheap; go on, read; and
when you are tired
then let its garment of letters
its body of words
its soul of rhythm
sink into space
like the last silent gesture of life.

Thinking in the Dark

It was dark,
the dark Red Fort, filled with a heap of darkness.
There were so many coloured lights,
halo after halo;
yet it was dark.
It swallowed up the Red Fort,
the thick, luxuriant darkness;
all those colourful lights
yet the view was dark, a dark black background
for everything and all.
On the streets, on every street
lights raced along, caught in the darkness;
particles of dust would rise illumined
in a halo of light, then be swallowed up.
Darkness drank
the cut, torn, racing, flaring, scattering
lights.
The crocodile of darkness
swam
in the ocean of darkness
with lightfish between its teeth.
The crocodile of darkness
breathed its fumes on the Red Fort.
The Red Fort was in the dark,
its towers, walls, gates were all
a heap of darkness.
But there was no doubt that it was there.
It was dark.
In the ocean of darkness,
deep in it,
the Red Fort.

Habit

The evening
enters the house through the roof.
I remove time
from my wrist
and put it neatly on the table.
Breathing a sigh of freedom
and relief
I take the oars of memory and dreams
and slide the boat of my perception
into the dark and murky waters.

By morning
I'll have carried the sun
on this boat of thought
and brought it here.
Then my wrist
will once again
be manacled with time
as I perform till evening
my hated chores.

Apology

No prayer marks my forehead,
no prayer-beads in my hand.
My experiences unwashed,
my grammar soiled and impure;
my letters, words
stained with tears, blood and dirt;
my forms unblessed, my style without ablutions.

How can I hold your holy name
on the tip of my tongue, O Lord!
Your wine so clean, so sweet, so pure;
my glass cracked, soiled, unclean.

Poem (3.11.66)

Today's my birthday.
I am thirty-eight today.
How quickly time passes!
I have lost nineteen teeth
and in my stomach sits Señora Caffein,
the residue of two hundred thousand cups of tea.
I have smoked three million cigarettes
and now my blood is sucked by
Lady Nicotine.

There are eight hundred and fifteen books
in the cupboards of my mind,
a pile of six and a half thousand newspapers
and so many albums containing photos
of faces, places.

One wife, three kids, two books, six notebooks, a few
friends; abuse, accusations, sweet-sounding words,
the empty-sounding drums of fame, notoriety;
the field of mind, soul, heart
where questions grow; for me
that is all that thirty-eight years have bestowed.

The books lying on the shelf want to read me
The blank page wants to write me
A few photographs want to cover my eyes
and some vague poems want to emerge
covered in paper
Cigarettes and tea want some more of me to consume
My life wants to live me a bit more
The mind wants to burst
Time wants to pass
Everyone wants something of me.

This thirty-ninth winter
has also brought some demands.

I wish it did not have bills
in its hand but receipts
or a perfume-laden envelope at least;
oxygen, love, some tulips
or a new book of songs
from one of my friends
or, laced in blood, the answers
to my questioning:
some tally of useful and useless breaths,
some unheard melody, some unseen dream.
The body hears the knock of the thirty-ninth winter.
The fireplace of thought
is searching out my bones for dry fuel
and with it, my hoard of desires and hopes.
So my puppet limbs
can go on performing their dance
my heart keeps spinning thread
from the rays of new hope.

Time passes so quickly!
I am thirty-eight today.
It is my birthday.

In the Valley of Death

He was the first man amongst the dead
to conquer the dark valley of death;
he was the first to reach the valley of death.

But his domain was desolate,
there was nothing, only himself;
in the dark he had no shadow even
to keep him company.
In this virgin, spreading valley
he panicked.
To populate this new world
he began
quietly to bring, man after man,
the friends he had left behind.
And soon in death's valley
new colonies emerged.
The more the population grew
the more the loneliness grew.
Now, frightened by his
eternal loneliness he thinks
of how he can take millions with him from here,
how he might
smash the world with atomic hands
to erase all memory of the world he left behind
to break all limits
and make one world
of the living and the dead.

FAHMIDA RIAZ

Born in 1946 at Meeruth, India, she graduated from Sind University and married in 1965.

She has so far published two collections of verse and a book of prose poems. Fahmida Riaz shocked the Pakistan literary establishment with her volume **Badan Dareeda**, in which she explored sensual and overtly sexual themes. She lives in India.

Inhibition

This wayward virgin girl of my thought
is shy of speaking in front of strangers.
Hidden by the veil of her
vague expression
she passes by, her head bowed,
ever so quietly.

Truth

Truth, pleasures, self-reliance
All toys of clay
Can break in a moment

Yet how beautiful is the world,
pure as Mary, bright as lies.

Between You and Me

There is nothing between
you and me
but this blue sheet.
Yet why is this lonely mist
descending on my heart,
why this deep silence,
why is each moment shrinking?

What I have in my heart
extends beyond 'conventional relationship'.
This conventional relationship
peeps at us through the walls,
I cannot breathe freely,
I am restless!

Doll

She's small,
that's why she's so lovable.
Pouting lips and rosy cheeks,
she sits there staring
through her blue eyes.
You can play with her
whenever you please.

You can shut her up in a cupboard
or display her on the mantelpiece.
She has no thirst
on her little pouting lips.
Don't be put out
at the surprise in her blue eyes.
Put her to bed
and she will somehow fall asleep.

Voice of Stone

You met me on this lonely hill;
this is the peak of our meeting,
this the stone of my loyalty,
naked, wild, sad and desolate.

For centuries
I have stood, embracing it,
collecting your breath in a torn shawl,
my dress billowing in the wind's cruel current.
Still I cling to the sharp dagger-points of stone
which have pierced so deep into my heart
that my blood has stained everything
but for centuries
I have stood embracing it, embracing it.
And I send a message to you
with a soaring bird:
If you could see me,
would you not be happy?
Stones turn to glittering diamonds,
roses grow from stone.

Mohajir*

These blue and yellow balloons
burst of their own volition.

From the heights of improbability
the shreds of rubber
like dead skin
fell so rapidly.

These lifeless rubber pieces,
where will they find a home?
They do not like the earth,
they will not merge with it.
Each pure and clean drop of water
tells them that
the stream that's sprouted from the rock
will flow its own way.

The balloons are very unhappy
with earth and water.

* A word of Arabic origin, meaning 'immigrant', and used to
refer to those Muslims who migrated to Pakistan after the partition of
India.

She Is a Woman Impure

She is a woman impure
trapped in the cycle of blood
in the chain of years and months
burning in the fire of lust
seeking her pleasures
mistress of the devil
following his ways
towards that elusive goal
which has no route
that meeting of light and fire
which is so hard to find.
Boiling blood inside her veins
has torn her breasts,
the thorns on her way
have severed her womb,
on her body's shame
there is no shade of sanctity.
But, O gods who rule this earth,
you shall never see
this woman impure
with a prayer on her lips
as a supplicant at your door.

IFTIQAR ARIF

Born in 1943 in Lucknow, Arif is a romantic poet who has recently come to prominence. He has been a journalist and broadcaster; he now lives in London and is director of **Urdu Markaz** (the Urdu Centre) funded by the Third World Foundation.

Ignorance of the Wise

What does the jeweller know
What kind of flowers grow
In which soil
What kind of fragrance dwells
In which flowers?
What does the jeweller know?
He lives his life amongst stones
Amongst greedy merchants
What does the jeweller know!

All the Same

On the shores of the Nile
or the banks of some other river,
all armies are the same.
All swords are the same.
The light trampled on by hooves
spreads from river to gallows,
the dim fearful glow left out
in burnt-out tents – the same.
All landscapes are the same.
After such sights a silence reigns
a silence that swallows up
the terror of drumbeat, the pomp of standard.
Silence is the speech of complaint
the accent of protest.
It's nothing new; it's an old story;
In every story the anger of the silenced
is the same.
On the shores of the Nile
or the banks of some other river,
all armies are the same!

Sad Evenings

Strange people we
who live on promises!
The night we should
have spent in waking
we spent dreaming;
The name we should have
learnt to forget
we kept calling;
The game we should have won
we've gone on losing.
Strange people we
who live on promises!
No one cures our hurt pride
No balm for the wounded hours
Years have passed yet no miracles;
The flames of passion extinguished
The possessors of the bow are pierced
with arrows.
The wall of night waits in vain
for the sun's armies.
When will he come
for whom we wait?
How unfortunate we are
who wait!
How unfortunate we
who live on promises!

The Twelfth Man

In fine weather
numerous spectators come
to applaud their team
and raise their idols' esteem.
I, separate and alone,
salute the twelfth man.

What a strange player
is the twelfth man!
The game goes on,
the applause goes on,
the crowd roars
and he, alien to it all,
waits, waits
for that moment,
for that instant
when disaster strikes.
When he comes out to play,
to the sound of clapping,
some word of praise,
some shout of applause
may be raised in his name;
and he, too, becomes
respected like the rest.

But this happens seldom.
Yet it's said that
a player's relationship
with the game
is lifelong;
though this relationship
can also break,
the heart that sinks
with the last whistle
can also break.

You are a twelfth man,
Iftiqar:
You too wait
for that moment
when disaster strikes,
some calamity.
You too, Iftiqar Arif,
you too will sink,
you too will break.

MORE ABOUT PENGUINS, PELICANS, PEREGRINES AND PUFFINS

CLASSICS IN TRANSLATION
IN PENGUINS

☐ *Remembrance of Things Past* **Marcel Proust**
☐ Volume One: ***Swann's Way, Within a Budding Grove*** £7.50
☐ Volume Two: ***The Guermantes Way, Cities of the Plain*** £7.50
☐ Volume Three: ***The Captive, The Fugitive, Time Regained*** £7.50

Terence Kilmartin's acclaimed revised version of C. K. Scott Moncrieff's original translation, published in paperback for the first time.

☐ *The Canterbury Tales* **Geoffrey Chaucer** £2.50

'Every age is a Canterbury Pilgrimage . . . nor can a child be born who is not one of these characters of Chaucer' – William Blake

☐ *Gargantua & Pantagruel* **Rabelais** £3.95

The fantastic adventures of two giants through which Rabelais (1495–1553) caricatured his life and times in a masterpiece of exuberance and glorious exaggeration.

☐ *The Brothers Karamazov* **Fyodor Dostoevsky** £3.95

A detective story on many levels, profoundly involving the question of the existence of God, Dostoevsky's great drama of parricide and fraternal jealousy triumphantly fulfilled his aim: 'to find the man in man . . . [to] depict all the depths of the human soul.'

☐ *Fables of Aesop* £1.95

This translation recovers all the old magic of fables in which, too often, the fox steps forward as the cynical hero and a lamb is an ass to lie down with a lion.

☐ *The Three Theban Plays* **Sophocles** £2.95

A new translation, by Robert Fagles, of *Antigone, Oedipus the King* and *Oedipus at Colonus*, plays all based on the legend of the royal house of Thebes.

CLASSICS IN TRANSLATION
IN PENGUINS

☐ **The Treasure of the City of Ladies**
Christine de Pisan £2.95

This practical survival handbook for women (whether royal courtiers or prostitutes) paints a vivid picture of their lives and preoccupations in France, *c.* 1405. First English translation.

☐ **Berlin Alexanderplatz** **Alfred Döblin** £4.95

The picaresque tale of an ex-murderer's progress through underworld Berlin. 'One of the great experimental fictions ... the German equivalent of *Ulysses* and Dos Passos' *U.S.A.*' – *Time Out*

☐ **Metamorphoses** **Ovid** £2.50

The whole of Western literature has found inspiration in Ovid's poem, a golden treasury of myths and legends that are linked by the theme of transformation.

☐ **Darkness at Noon** **Arthur Koestler** £1.95

'Koestler approaches the problem of ends and means, of love and truth and social organization, through the thoughts of an Old Bolshevik, Rubashov, as he awaits death in a G.P.U. prison' – *New Statesman*

☐ **War and Peace** **Leo Tolstoy** £4.95

'A complete picture of human life;' wrote one critic, 'a complete picture of the Russia of that day; a complete picture of everything in which people place their happiness and greatness, their grief and humiliation.'

☐ **The Divine Comedy: 1 Hell** **Dante** £2.25

A new translation by Mark Musa, in which the poet is conducted by the spirit of Virgil down through the twenty-four closely described circles of hell.

ENGLISH AND AMERICAN LITERATURE IN PENGUINS

☐ *Emma* **Jane Austen**   £1.10

'I am going to take a heroine whom no one but myself will much like,'
declared Jane Austen of Emma, her most spirited and controversial
heroine in a comedy of self-deceit and self-discovery.

☐ *Tender is the Night* **F. Scott Fitzgerald**   £2.95

Fitzgerald worked on seventeen different versions of this novel, and
its obsessions – idealism, beauty, dissipation, alcohol and insanity –
were those that consumed his own marriage and his life.

☐ *The Life of Johnson* **James Boswell**   £2.25

Full of gusto, imagination, conversation and wit, Boswell's immortal
portrait of Johnson is as near a novel as a true biography can be, and
still regarded by many as the finest 'life' ever written. This shortened
version is based on the 1799 edition.

☐ *A House and its Head* **Ivy Compton-Burnett**   £3.95

In a novel 'as trim and tidy as a hand-grenade' (as Pamela Hansford
Johnson put it), Ivy Compton-Burnett penetrates the facade of a
conventional, upper-class Victorian family to uncover a chasm of
violent emotions – jealousy, pain, frustration and sexual passion.

☐ *The Trumpet Major* **Thomas Hardy**   £1.25

Although a vein of unhappy unrequited love runs through this novel,
Hardy also draws on his warmest sense of humour to portray
Wessex village life at the time of the Napoleonic wars.

☐ *The Complete Poems of Hugh MacDiarmid*

☐ Volume One   £8.95
☐ Volume Two   £8.95

The definitive edition of work by the greatest Scottish poet since
Robert Burns, edited by his son Michael Grieve, and W. R. Aitken.

ENGLISH AND AMERICAN
LITERATURE IN PENGUINS

☐ *Main Street* **Sinclair Lewis** £3.95

The novel that added an immortal chapter to the literature of America's Mid-West, *Main Street* contains the comic essence of Main Streets everywhere.

☐ *The Compleat Angler* **Izaak Walton** £2.50

A celebration of the countryside, and the superiority of those in 1653, as now, who love *quietnesse, vertue* and, above all, *Angling.* 'No fish, however coarse, could wish for a doughtier champion than Izaak Walton' – Lord Home

☐ *The Portrait of a Lady* **Henry James** £2.50

'One of the two most brilliant novels in the language', according to F. R. Leavis, James's masterpiece tells the story of a young American heiress, prey to fortune-hunters but not without a will of her own.

☐ *Hangover Square* **Patrick Hamilton** £3.50

Part love story, part thriller, and set in the publands of London's Earls Court, this novel caught the conversational tone of a whole generation in the uneasy months before the Second World War.

☐ *The Rainbow* **D. H. Lawrence** £2.50

Written between *Sons and Lovers* and *Women in Love, The Rainbow* covers three generations of Brangwens, a yeoman family living on the borders of Nottinghamshire.

☐ *Vindication of the Rights of Woman*
   Mary Wollstonecraft £2.95

Although Walpole once called her 'a hyena in petticoats', Mary Wollstonecraft's vision was such that modern feminists continue to go back and debate the arguments so powerfully set down here.

PENGUIN OMNIBUSES

☐ **Victorian Villainies**   £4.95

Fraud, murder, political intrigue and horror are the ingredients of these four Victorian thrillers, selected by Hugh Greene and Graham Greene.

☐ **The Balkan Trilogy** Olivia Manning   £5.95

This acclaimed trilogy – *The Great Fortune, The Spoilt City* and *Friends and Heroes* – is the portrait of a marriage, and an exciting recreation of civilian life in the Second World War. 'It amuses, it diverts, and it informs' – Frederick Raphael

☐ **The Penguin Collected Stories of Isaac Bashevis Singer**   £4.95

Forty-seven marvellous tales of Jewish magic, faith and exile. 'Never was the Nobel Prize more deserved . . . He belongs with the giants' – *Sunday Times*

☐ **The Penguin Essays of George Orwell**   £4.95

Famous pieces on 'The Decline of the English Murder', 'Shooting an Elephant', political issues and P. G. Wodehouse feature in this edition of forty-one essays, criticism and sketches – all classics of English prose.

☐ **Further Chronicles of Fairacre** 'Miss Read'   £3.95

Full of humour, warmth and charm, these four novels – *Miss Clare Remembers, Over the Gate, The Fairacre Festival* and *Emily Davis* – make up an unforgettable picture of English village life.

☐ **The Penguin Complete Sherlock Holmes** Sir Arthur Conan Doyle   £5.95

With the fifty-six classic short stories, plus *A Study in Scarlet, The Sign of Four, The Hound of the Baskervilles* and *The Valley of Fear*, this volume contains the remarkable career of Baker Street's most famous resident.

PENGUIN OMNIBUSES

☐ *Life with Jeeves* **P. G. Wodehouse**   £3.50

Containing *Right Ho, Jeeves, The Inimitable Jeeves* and *Very Good, Jeeves!* in which Wodehouse lures us, once again, into the evergreen world of Bertie Wooster, his terrifying Aunt Agatha, his man Jeeves and other eggs, good and bad.

☐ *The Penguin Book of Ghost Stories*   £4.95

An anthology to set the spine tingling, including stories by Zola, Kleist, Sir Walter Scott, M. R. James, Elizabeth Bowen and A. S. Byatt.

☐ *The Penguin Book of Horror Stories*   £4.95

Including stories by Maupassant, Poe, Gautier, Conan Doyle, L. P. Hartley and Ray Bradbury, in a selection of the most horrifying horror from the eighteenth century to the present day.

☐ *The Penguin Complete Novels of Jane Austen*   £5.95

Containing the seven great novels: *Sense and Sensibility, Pride and Prejudice, Mansfield Park, Emma, Northanger Abbey, Persuasion* and *Lady Susan*.

☐ *Perfick, Perfick!* **H. E. Bates**   £3.95

The adventures of the irrepressible Larkin family, in four novels: *The Darling Buds of May, A Breath of French Air, When the Green Woods Laugh* and *Oh! To Be in England*.

☐ *Famous Trials*
   Harry Hodge and James H. Hodge   £3.95

From Madeleine Smith to Dr Crippen and Lord Haw-Law, this volume contains the most sensational murder and treason trials, selected by John Mortimer from the classic Penguin Famous Trials series.

PENGUIN TRAVEL BOOKS

☐ *Arabian Sands* **Wilfred Thesiger**   £3.50

'In the tradition of Burton, Doughty, Lawrence, Philby and Thomas, it is, very likely, the book about Arabia to end all books about Arabia' – *Daily Telegraph*

☐ *The Flight of Ikaros* **Kevin Andrews**   £3.50

'He also is in love with the country . . . but he sees the other side of that dazzling medal or moon . . . If you want some truth about Greece, here it is' – Louis MacNeice in the *Observer*

☐ *D. H. Lawrence and Italy*   £4.95

In *Twilight in Italy, Sea and Sardinia* and *Etruscan Places*, Lawrence recorded his impressions while living, writing and travelling in 'one of the most beautiful countries in the world'.

☐ *Maiden Voyage* **Denton Welch**   £3.50

Opening during his last term at public school, from which the author absconded, *Maiden Voyage* turns into a brilliantly idiosyncratic account of China in the 1930s.

☐ *The Grand Irish Tour* **Peter Somerville-Large**   £4.95

The account of a year's journey round Ireland. 'Marvellous . . . describes to me afresh a landscape I thought I knew' – Edna O'Brien in the *Observer*

☐ *Slow Boats to China* **Gavin Young**   £3.95

On an ancient steamer, a cargo dhow, a Filipino kumpit and twenty more agreeably cranky boats, Gavin Young sailed from Piraeus to Canton in seven crowded and colourful months. 'A pleasure to read' – Paul Theroux

PENGUIN TRAVEL BOOKS

☐ *The Kingdom by the Sea* **Paul Theroux**   **£2.50**

1982, the year of the Falklands War and the Royal Baby, was the ideal time, Theroux found, to travel round the coast of Britain and surprise the British into talking about themselves. 'He describes it all brilliantly and honestly' – Anthony Burgess

☐ *One's Company* **Peter Fleming**   **£2.95**

His journey to China as special correspondent to *The Times* in 1933. 'One reads him for literary delight . . . But, he is also an observer of penetrating intellect' – Vita Sackville West

☐ *The Traveller's Tree* **Patrick Leigh Fermor**   **£3.95**

'A picture of the Indies more penetrating and original than any that has been presented before' – *Observer*

☐ *The Path to Rome* **Hilaire Belloc**   **£3.95**

'The only book I ever wrote for love,' is how Belloc described the wonderful blend of anecdote, humour and reflection that makes up the story of his pilgrimage to Rome.

☐ *The Light Garden of the Angel King* **Peter Levi**   **£2.95**

Afghanistan has been a wild rocky highway for nomads and merchants, Alexander the Great, Buddhist monks, great Moghul conquerors and the armies of the Raj. Here, quite brilliantly, Levi writes about their journeys and his own.

☐ *Among the Russians* **Colin Thubron**   **£2.95**

'The Thubron approach to travelling has an integrity that belongs to another age' – Dervla Murphy in the *Irish Times*. 'A magnificent achievement' – Nikolai Tolstoy

PENGUIN BOOKS OF POETRY